MONTANA SEAL UNDERCOVER DADDY

BROTHERHOOD PROTECTORS #9

ELLE JAMES

TWISTED PAGE INC

Ebook ISBN: 978-1-62695-149-5

Print ISBN: 978-1-62695-150-1

For my friends who help me when I need brainstorming help. For my editor who drops everything to edit at the last minute. For my beta readers: Carmen, Kim, Fedora and Phyllis who jump in when I beg for help. For my family who puts up with me when I'm 24/7 at my computer pounding away on the keyboard. You are the ones who help me make it happen, and for that I'm eternally grateful. I love you all!

AUTHOR'S NOTE

Enjoy other military books by Elle James

Brotherhood Protector Series
Montana SEAL (#1)
Bride Protector SEAL (#2)
Montana D-Force (#3)
Cowboy D-Force (#4)
Montana Ranger (#5)
Montana Dog Soldier (#6)
Montana SEAL Daddy (#7)
Montana Ranger's Wedding Vow (#8)
Montana SEAL Undercover Daddy (#9)
Montana SEAL Friendly Fire (#10)
Montana SEAL's Bride (#11) TBD
Montana Rescue

Visit ellejames.com for more titles and release dates
For hot cowboys, visit her alter ego Myla Jackson at
mylajackson.com
and join Elle James and Myla Jackson's Newsletter at
Newsletter

CHAPTER 1

THE INCESSANT VIBRATION of the cellphone on her nightstand woke Kate Phillips from a melatonin-induced deep sleep. She would have ignored the urgent ringing if it hadn't been the third time in as many minutes that it had gone off.

She rolled over and blinked to clear the sleep from her eyes.

Unknown Caller.

Then a text flashed across the screen.

IT'S RACHEL. ANSWER YOUR PHONE. 911!

The phone vibrated again.

Kate frowned and hit the button to receive the call. "Rachel? What's wrong?"

"I need you to open your door." Her younger sister's voice sounded strained, almost desperate.

"Why?" Kate sat up in her bed and untangled her legs from the sheets.

"Open your door, Kate. Now!"

She dropped her feet to the ground, grabbed her robe from the end of the bed and rushed toward her apartment door. "Okay, okay. Keep your pants on."

"Hurry. It's very important. And don't hang up yet. I have to know."

"I'm at the door," she said. "Unlocking." She fumbled with the two deadbolts and the chain, and looked through the peephole before she twisted the lock on the handle. She didn't see anyone standing outside the door. "Where are you? I don't see anyone outside."

"Just open the door!" Rachel cried.

If Kate wasn't mistaken, her twin sister's voice caught on a sob.

"What's wrong, sweetie?" she said as she pulled the door open and nearly fell over the bundle lying on the ground at her feet.

"Is she there?" Rachel asked, her voice a shaky whisper. "Kate, please. Tell me. Is she there?"

"Is who..." The bundle on the ground moved and rolled over. A sweet, pink face turned toward her, and silky, blond hair spilled from beneath the edge of a child's blanket. "Oh, sweet Jesus," Kate whispered. "Lyla?"

"Oh, thank God!" Rachel cried. "She's still there. She didn't wander off." Rachel's sobs filled Kate's ear.

She squatted next to her sister's three-year-old daughter and brushed a strand of golden hair from her face.

The child remained asleep, her cherubic face peaceful, despite being left on Kate's doorstep.

Kate looked around, fully expecting to see Rachel.

She rarely went anywhere without Lyla in tow. Her sister was nowhere to be seen. "Rachel, where are you?"

"I can't say." She sniffed. "Oh, Kate. I'm afraid. I'm doing the only thing I know to keep Lyla safe. You have to help me."

"Slow down, Rachel," Kate said, careful not to wake Lyla. "I need to put the phone down to bring Lyla into the apartment. Hold on."

"No! Kate, don't put the phone down. I only have a moment. You need you to listen."

"Okay," Kate said. "I'm listening."

"Take Lyla. Get out of your apartment. Take her to Eagle Rock, Montana, to a man named Hank Patterson. He has a protection agency. He'll help you protect Lyla. And Kate, you have to make everyone believe Lyla is your little girl. No one can know she was mine. No one."

"Rachel, what's going on? Do you need me to call the police?"

"No! You can't. Please, don't. Involving the police will only make things worse. If you love me and if you love my baby girl, you'll do this. It's the only way to keep her safe."

"What about you, Rachel?" Kate gripped the phone so tightly, her hand cramped. "Who's going to keep you safe?"

"Until I figure this out, I have to disappear. It's the only way. So, please, in your own way, you and Lyla needed to disappear. Hank will help you accomplish that."

"Rachel, you're scaring me. Where's Myles? Why isn't he helping?"

"I can't talk right now," Rachel said, her voice catching on what sounded like a sob.

"I'm your big sister." Big sister by five minutes. But still the older of the two. "You know you can tell me anything."

"I know, Kate, but there are some things better left unsaid. In this case, the less you know the better. Keep Lyla safe. Change her name. Change your name. Do whatever it takes to make her your own."

"For how long, Rachel?" Kate clutched the phone to her ear, afraid to hear her sister's answer.

"I don't know if I'll be able to come back."

"What do you mean?"

"As long as I'm anywhere near her, Lyla is in danger. In order to keep her safe, I had to leave her." Her voice hitched. "You have to be her mother. You're her only chance."

"Rachel, you're scaring me."

"Believe me," Rachel said, "I'm terrified. Not so much for me, but Lyla is caught up in this mess. They'll use her to get to me."

"Who will use her?" Kate asked.

"I don't have time to go into it. I have to run."

"Rachel, I don't know anything about little girls. I barely know Lyla."

"You look enough like me. The important thing is for you to be Lyla's mother. She has to believe you're her mom so that everyone she comes into contact with believes you're her mother."

"You don't understand," Kate stared down at the sleeping child. "I don't know how to be a mother. You were always the nurturing one."

"Just love her. Lyla makes it easy."

"Rachel, just come back. I'll protect you."

"I can't. Lyla deserves a real life. The way things are right now, I can't give that to her."

"Rachel—"

"I love you, Kate."

"I love you too, Rachel."

"Go to Montana. Find Hank. Protect my baby."

"Please, don't hang up," Kate begged.

The call ended.

Tears slipped down Kate's face as she stared down at the cellphone.

The small bundle lying at her feet moved.

Lyla blinked her eyes open. "Where's Sid Sloth?" she mumbled, her tiny voice hoarse with sleep.

"I'm sorry?" Kate didn't understand.

Lyla rooted around in the blanket and pulled from the jumble a stuffed animal that looked suspiciously like a sloth and tucked it beneath her chin. Then she yawned and closed her eyes again.

Headlights glared in the parking lot of her townhouse apartment. A dark sedan pulled into a parking space, and the lights blinked off.

Kate's heart leaped. She gathered Lyla and her blankets into her arms, and hunkering low, swung her into the apartment and closed the door. She laid the entire bundle on the floor and quickly spun around to close the door.

Footsteps sounded on the sidewalk in front of the apartment.

Kate reached out to turn the button on the door handle lock as the steps stopped. She eased the deadbolt in place as quietly as possible.

The handle moved as if someone on the other side might be trying it.

Her pulse hammered so hard it beat against her eardrums. She waited by the door, afraid to move, not knowing what to expect.

She wanted to call her sister back and ask her what the hell she'd gotten into. The last she'd heard from her sister was a phone call a couple of months before.

Rachel and her husband, Myles, had moved to a small town in Wyoming three years ago, when Rachel was pregnant with their first child. They were concerned about raising their daughter in the hustle and bustle of Los Angeles where Rachel and Kate had grown up. With drive-by shootings, horrendous traffic and pollution, it wasn't the ideal place to raise a child.

Rachel's husband had found a job as a communications specialist with a church in a small community. They'd seemed happy. But lately, Rachel's phone calls were short and not very newsy.

Kate had been so busy with her own career, she hadn't thought much about it. She'd figured Rachel was busy being a full-time mom.

When her husband of ten years divorced her, Kate gave up on the idea of marriage and children. Her husband had never wanted children. Though she'd later learned he never wanted children with her. As soon as they divorced, he married his pregnant secretary.

Kate had thrown herself into her career in freelance news reporting and left the marriage and mommy business to her little sister, who'd seemed to be doing it the right way.

Until now.

Kate stared down at the bundle on the floor.

Lyla slept on.

A knock on the door jerked Kate back to her predicament.

She lifted Lyla, blankets and all, carried her into the bedroom, shut the door and locked it. Then she grabbed her cellphone and dialed 911.

"You've reached the emergency department. Please state your emergency."

Kate had never called 911 in her life. What did she say? "There's someone at my door," she blurted.

"Are they trying to break in?"

"I don't know. But it's late, and I'm not expecting anyone."

"Ma'am, I'm sending someone over right away. Are you somewhere relatively safe?"

"I'm in my bedroom with the door locked."

"You might also go into the bathroom and lock the door. Please stay on the line until help arrives."

"I will." She laid the phone on the sleeping child, gathered her in her arms and carried her into the bathroom and locked the door.

With nowhere else to sit, she closed the toilet lid and

sat on the seat, holding Lyla and rocking her gently, more to calm herself than the sleeping child.

She strained to hear what was going on outside her bathroom and bedroom. The doors and walls muffled sounds. Was that the sound of the wood splitting on a doorjamb?

Her heart hammering against her ribs so hard she could barely breathe, Kate held Lyla tighter and prayed the police would arrive before whoever had just broken the deadbolt on her front door made it through the measly lock on the bedroom door, and then the equally pathetic lock on her bathroom door.

Kate laid Lyla in the bathtub. She had to do something to protect her sister's child. Waiting for help that might not make it in time wasn't good enough. She pulled down the curtain rod and thought about jamming it between the walls over the door. She shook her head. That little bit of flimsy metal wouldn't hold under the weight of a full-grown man. Instead, she took off one end of it and held the other in a firm grip.

If her intruder made his way through her apartment and into the bathroom before the police arrived, Kate would be ready.

She'd never hit anyone before in her life. But she'd do whatever it took to protect Lyla.

A crashing sound heralded the destruction of her bedroom lock and doorframe.

Kate stood back from the bathroom door, holding the curtain rod in both hands like a baseball bat. When the man shoved through the door, she'd hit him hard and fast. She'd have the element of surprise on her side. He wouldn't know it was coming.

Footsteps sounded in her bedroom. She was eternally grateful for the wood floors in her apartment. She knew exactly when he stopped in front of the bathroom door.

She held her breath, tightening her grip on the curtain rod as she pulled it back and stood like a baseball player ready to slam a home run.

The door handle jiggled, making Kate jump.

Then nothing.

She braced herself for what would come next.

In the distance, the sound of a siren wailed, moving closer.

Please hurry, she prayed silently and bent her knees, ready.

Then the door exploded inward.

A man charged through the door, dressed in black, with a black ski mask covering his face. He carried a gun in his hand.

Scared out of her mind, Kate didn't hesitate. She swung that curtain rod as hard as she could right for the man's head.

The metal rod connected with the intruder's face, making a crunching sound as if she'd broken his nose.

The man fell to his knees, clutching at his nose, and moaned. Blood seeped through the knitted mask onto his hands.

All Kate could think was that the man was still upright and able to continue his attack.

She swung again and again.

The masked man raised his arms to protect his head. Then he grabbed the rod.

Kate pulled hard, knowing that if she released it, he'd be able to turn it on her. She couldn't let that happen. Lyla need her to protect her.

Refusing to let go, Kate swung out her foot and put all her kickboxing training into one mighty sidekick.

She caught the man in the side of the head.

For a moment, her kick didn't seem to have done anything.

Then her attacker let go of the rod and tipped over sideways.

Kate grabbed Lyla and ran out of her apartment into the parking lot and was almost run over by a cop car.

The police officer slammed on his brakes, skidded sideways and came to a stop inches away from Kate and Lyla.

The police officer jumped out of his vehicle and pulled his gun out of the holster. "Which apartment?"

She pointed to the open door.

"Get into the squad car until my backup arrives." The officer didn't wait to see that Kate made it into his vehicle. He ran for the apartment, speaking into the radio clipped to his shoulder, and paused at the side of the door.

Kate slid into the back seat of the police car and held Lyla in her arms.

Another siren wailed nearby, and soon, another police car arrived.

With two officers now on the scene, they entered Kate's apartment.

Watching through the window, Kate held her breath, hoping they'd caught the guy. She'd never been so frightened in her entire life. And not for herself, but for the innocent little girl lying sleeping in her arms.

Kate stared down at the child's golden hair so much like hers and her sister's. Kate and Rachel were twins separated by only five minutes. Now, there was a world between them, and Kate didn't know where to look for her sister. "Oh, Rachel, what's going on?"

CHAPTER 2

"CHUCK, I have a new assignment for you." Hank Patterson didn't preface the telephone call with niceties like "Hello." He got right down to business.

His boss's directness was one of the things former Navy SEAL Chuck Johnson appreciated about Hank, the founder of the Brotherhood Protectors agency and the main reason he'd jumped ship from the DEA. Not only was he direct, Hank was a Navy SEAL as well. And once a SEAL, always a SEAL. The bonds between SEALs were unbroken and forever.

Chuck had just left Daphne and Boomer's house. After spending the evening babysitting their baby, Maya, he was ready to head to the bed and breakfast where he'd taken up residence. He'd shower, drink a beer and maybe drown his sorrows for another night.

Hank's call, a welcome distraction, got his blood moving. He'd much rather work than go back to his little room by himself, especially after holding and cuddling baby Maya.

If Daphne and Boomer weren't so crazy happy in love, Chuck might have fought to win Daphne's affections. Knowing how much Daphne loved Boomer made Chuck realize he hadn't been in love with Daphne at all. If anything, he'd been more in love with Maya and pretending to be a father to the baby, than he was in love with Daphne. Daphne had been more like a daughter to him. He'd never really felt more than a fatherly or brotherly affection for Maya's mother.

Chuck's problem was that despite having sworn off family and relationships for so long, he really longed to have another child and a woman to come home to. Not to replace the loved ones he'd lost, but in addition to them.

Chuck slowed his truck, preparing to turn if he needed to. "What's the assignment?"

"I need you to come to the ranch. Your assignment is waiting here."

"On it." Chuck made a U-turn in the middle of the deserted highway and applied his foot heavily to the accelerator, speeding his way to White Oak Ranch where Hank had set up the headquarters for his brainchild, Brotherhood Protectors.

Chuck needed the work to distract him from his longing to be a father to Maya. Not that Daphne was keeping him from the baby he'd been with since her birth. But the child needed to bond with her father who had only recently come into her life. Chuck didn't need to muddy Maya's waters.

If he wanted children, he could find his own wife and have babies. Borrowing another family's children... well, he'd just have to stay clear of those situations.

Surely, he could find a woman who wouldn't mind marrying a man past his prime and heading unflinchingly toward the mid-century mark. He wasn't old, but women of a childbearing age might consider him too old to father their children.

Why he was even thinking about a wife and children was self-defeating. He'd been a bachelor for so long, he would be terrible at a relationship.

He arrived within fifteen minutes of the call and pulled up to the sprawling rock and cedar house that had been built with a bunker beneath it, housing the armory, computer system and conference room for the brotherhood.

Chuck dropped down from his truck and climbed the steps to the front porch.

Hank met him at the door and opened it to let him into the wide-open living room with the cathedral ceilings and stone fireplace.

Sadie smiled at him from across the room. She carried her baby Emma in her arms. "Hey, Chuck. Would you care for a drink? I was just going to make tea for our guest."

Normally, Chuck would have accepted a beer, but he didn't know when his new assignment would begin, and he wanted an absolutely clear head going in. "No, thank you."

Hank waved Chuck toward a seat in the living room. "You might want to sit down for a moment. Your client will be out shortly."

Chuck shook his head. "Thanks, but I've been sitting in a rocking chair for the past three hours."

Hank grinned. "Practicing for your old age?"

Chuck laughed. "Not quite, though some would say I am. I just left Boomer and Daphne's house. I kept Maya while they went out for date night."

"Makes sense. You've been with Maya since she was born. She's comfortable with you and Daphne knows you." He glanced toward Sadie, his wife. "Sadie and I still find it difficult to leave Emma with anyone." He winked at Chuck. "I'll have to keep you in mind."

"Do," Chuck offered. "I'm pretty good with babies. I can change a diaper in five seconds flat." He wrinkled his nose. "Well, depending on the damage."

"You're hired," Sadie said. "Oh, wait. You're already hired as a Brotherhood Protector."

"And your skills with children is part of the reason I chose you for this assignment," Hank said.

Chuck frowned. "Why?"

"You will have two clients. And you're pretty much conducting the same kind of operation you led with the DEA when you were assigned to protect Daphne and her baby."

"Witness protection?" Chuck guessed.

"Not quite, but close. One of your clients is a marketing executive." Hank looked past Chuck. "Ah, here they are now." He held out his hand. "Kate, let me introduce one of the newest members of my team, Chuck Johnson."

Chuck turned toward a striking woman with sandy-blond hair and clear, blue eyes. Her skin was tanned, and she wore a white blouse, khaki slacks and leather loafers.

"Chuck, meet Kate Phillips," Hank said.

Kate held out her hand. "Thank you for coming so quickly. I didn't want to show up anywhere else around here until I had my cover firmly in place."

"What cover?" Chuck asked.

She frowned. "You, of course." The woman darted a glance toward Hank. "I did specify the man had to be of above-average intelligence, did I not?"

Hank's lips twisted. "Don't let all those muscles fool you. Chuck is one of the smartest and most mature men on my team."

Chuck leaned toward Kate. "That's code for old." He inhaled and caught the scent that could only be described as plumeria. He hadn't smelled that scent in a very long time. Anne had loved the aroma of plumeria. Whenever he was in Hawaii, Chuck picked up bottles of lotion with that scent.

She'd still had one left when she'd...

Chuck shook himself out of the past and held out a hand. "Nice to meet you, Ms. Phillips."

"Please, call me Kate," she insisted, her grip firm though her hands were small.

In keeping with his promise to himself to steer clear of relationships, he shook his head. "If you don't mind, I'd like to keep it on a professional level."

Kate shot a glance toward Hank. "Perhaps Mr. Johnson isn't so perfect for this job after all."

"I can do anything," Chuck protested.

She arched an eyebrow. "Can you do as requested? Because I need someone who can follow orders as well as give out a few of his own."

His back stiffened. "I've done my share of following and giving orders, Kate." If he put too much emphasis on her name, so be it. She'd questioned his ability to do a job.

Her eyes narrowed on Chuck, and then she faced Hank again. "My sister recommended you. Is this the best that you have? Because I need the best. I need someone who will lay down his life for us."

Hank touched her arm. "It's all right, Kate. With Chuck, you'll be in good hands. And he has the perfect skill set for the job."

Chuck frowned. "You keep saying that. I assume any one of your men has the same skill set I do."

"They do...for the most part." Hank grinned. "You have one more skill most of the others do not."

Trying to figure it out himself, Chuck gave up. "And that is?"

Sadie said, "You have daddy skills. I knew you were the right man for the job as soon as Kate mentioned that requirement."

"Requirement?" Chuck glanced from Sadie to Hank, and then to Kate. "I don't understand."

"Mama?" a little voice called out.

Everyone in the room turned toward the sound.

A little girl with bright, blond hair emerged from the hallway leading to the bedrooms.

Kate hurried toward the child. "Lyla, you should be asleep." She patted the child's back awkwardly.

"I can't find Sid." Lyla looked up at Kate. "I can't sleep without Sid."

"Who's Sid?" Chuck asked. "Is there another child?"

Kate shook her head. "Sid is Lyla's stuffed sloth." She knelt on the floor in front of Lyla. "Did you look under the covers?"

She nodded. "I want *you* to look," she whispered.

Chuck's heart constricted. His Sarah hadn't been much younger than this little girl. Seeing Lyla standing there in a T-shirt too big for her little body reminded him so much of Sarah. His chest squeezed so hard, he could barely breathe.

Kate took Lyla's hand and faced Chuck. "This is Lyla. She's the reason I need someone with daddy skills. I need to blend into wherever I land. And that means we have to look like a family. Mama, Daddy and Lyla. Anywhere we go, we have to pretend we're a unit. No one can know she isn't mine."

Panic tightened his throat. Chuck held up his hand. "I can't do this."

"Can't, or won't?" Kate hit him with that direct stare. "I need one hundred percent commitment."

"Why do you need protection?" Chuck bit out. "What are you afraid of?"

"I'm afraid of whoever broke into my apartment and tried to take Lyla. I don't know who they are or why they were after her, but I have to keep her safe. I promised."

"Promised who?" Chuck asked.

Her lips firmed into a narrow line. "That doesn't matter. What matters is that we protect Lyla in the best way we can. I need everyone who comes into contact with her...with us...to think we're a family. The people looking for her will be looking for a lone woman and child, not a family of three."

Chuck studied Kate, his eyes narrowing. "How do we know you didn't..." he lowered his voice to a point Lyla wouldn't hear or understand, "How do we know you didn't kidnap Lyla? Is she even yours to hide?" His gaze shifted from Kate to Hank. "Do you know?"

Hank's lips quirked. "You have a good point, Chuck." He smiled at Kate. "Kate is actually Lyla's aunt. Her sister left her on her doorstep and disappeared."

Chuck crossed his arms over his chest. "And how do you know Kate didn't off her sister to steal her daughter?"

Lyla leaned her cheek against Kate's leg.

Kate's eyes filled. She blinked several times and lifted her chin. "I love my sister. I wouldn't *off* her." She patted Lyla's head, without picking up the child.

Chuck couldn't understand why the woman wasn't taking the child into her arms to reassure and comfort her. Impatience and concern for the little girl won out. Chuck bent to Lyla. "Hey, do you want me to hold you?"

The child stared up at Chuck, clutching her hands against her chest. Her big, blue eyes showed fear at first, but then she yawned and held up her arms.

Chuck lifted Lyla into his arms and held her close. He gently rubbed her back until she laid her head on his shoulder and closed her eyes. She drew in a deep breath and slept.

Kate's eyes rounded. "How did you do that?"

"Do what?" Chuck asked.

Sadie chuckled. "The man has a magic touch with small children. Emma took to him from the moment he held her in his arms."

Hank nodded. "Exactly like Lyla just did. That's why I knew he was the right man for the job."

Chuck ignored them all and carried the sleeping Lyla back down the hallway.

"Second door on the right," Sadie called out.

He found the door and entered the room with a full-sized bed in the middle of the floor decorated in light blues and grays.

A small child's blanket lay in the middle of the bed. He'd found the right room.

Careful not to wake Lyla, he laid her down, covered her with the blanket. He found Sid, the sloth, hiding under a pillow, and slipped the stuffed animal beneath her arm. Then he backed away slowly.

At the door to the bedroom, Chuck paused to look back at Lyla and wondered what his own little girl would have looked like at that age. Sarah never made it to three.

His heart contracted, squeezing hard in his chest.

Lyla lay sleeping, her silky blond hair fanning out around her on the pillow, her stuffed animal tucked beneath her arm.

He'd just convinced himself the best course of action for him was to steer clear of women with small children. They reminded him too much of what he was missing, and he got too attached.

He still missed being with Maya every day, like he

had when she and Daphne were under his care in witness protection.

But if he didn't do this job, who would? He thought through the other men on the Brotherhood Protectors team. Only a couple had been around kids. And those were on other jobs.

Chuck stared at Lyla lying there, so innocent, so vulnerable, and he struggled inwardly.

"I'm sorry I was rude," a voice said behind him.

He didn't have to turn to know it was Kate. "It's all right. You're worried about your niece and your sister."

"You were very good with her." She moved up beside him. "I'm afraid I don't know much about children. I left all of that up to my sister. While she was raising Lyla, I was concentrating on my career. I didn't know what I was missing, and I liked it that way."

Chuck understood all too well. He knew what he'd been missing after his wife and daughter died and, at times, wished he could forget. He loved children.

When Daphne had given birth to Maya during the time they were under his protection, he wasn't sure he could handle being so close. But Maya came along and wrapped herself around his little finger so fast he didn't know he was in love with her until it was too late. Now that Maya's father was back in the picture and one of the Brotherhood Protectors, Chuck had made the decision to back out and give them time to bond as a family.

She locked gazes with him. "I need someone who can help me protect her."

Chuck nodded.

"Lyla needs someone who understands what she

needs." Kate sighed. "I'm not sure I'm that person. Frankly, I need help."

"She's lost her mother, for all intents and purposes. Until your sister returns, she needs stability in her life. She needs to know she's safe and loved."

Kate stared at Lyla, her brows dipping into a concerned frown. "My sister moved away when Lyla was born. I barely know my niece. I don't know how to take care of a child."

"It's not hard," Chuck said.

"For you, maybe." She turned to face Chuck. "So, will you help me?"

"A moment ago, you didn't think I was the right man for the job."

"Then I saw you with Lyla. She took to you right away. And Hank says you're a Navy SEAL, one of the best." She touched his arm.

A shock of electricity shot through his nerves. He glanced at the hand on his arm.

She pulled back her hand. "Please," she said softly.

His gaze rose to connect with hers.

She had blue eyes, just like Lyla's. "Lyla looks like you," Chuck said.

Kate laughed. "She does. But then I look like my sister. We're twins."

Kate's blond hair was a shade darker than Lyla's, but the eyes were unmistakably sky blue and matched the child's perfectly. Her skin glowed with a healthy tan, and when she smiled, her entire face lit up.

Beautiful.

Not in the runway model way, but in a real, girl-next-door, simple loveliness.

Chuck shook his head. And there were two of them?

"I'll double whatever Hank pays you," Kate said, her eyes wide and pleading.

"No."

Kate's shoulders sagged. "I get it. I was rude. If it helps, my father was military. I have great respect for our country's men and women in uniform."

"No," Chuck said. "You don't have to pay me double. I'll do the job."

"But Lyla already likes you. It makes sense for you to be the one...wait...what?" She stared at him with her pretty brows drawing together. "You will?"

He nodded. "I will. When do you need me to start?"

"Now," she replied, without hesitation. "We need to start now. Before I show up in town in broad daylight."

"Then we start now." He tipped his head toward Lyla. "No use waking her until we figure out the logistics."

Kate threw her arms around Chuck's neck. "Thank you."

Her body felt warm and soft against his. Chuck wrapped his arms around her middle as if they belonged there. She was just the right height. Not too tall or short, and her muscles were firm. He drew in a deep breath, inhaling the subtle scent of her perfume. He liked it. And he liked the way she felt pressed against him. A little too much for having just met her.

She was now his client. Other than pretending to be

her husband and the father of her child, he had to keep their relationship professional.

He set her away from him and dropped his hands to his sides. "If we're going to pretend to be a family, we need a place to stay. The bed and breakfast I'm renting now isn't big enough for the three of us. Let's talk with Hank. He's more familiar with the area than I am."

Kate rubbed her arms, her cheeks flushing a pretty pink. "Of course. We should talk with Hank. He'll know where we can go."

"In the meantime, we need to come up with a cover story. Since I've been here a few weeks, folks might have noticed I've been alone. They'll wonder how a wife and child came from out of nowhere."

Her eyebrows drew together, and her gaze sharpened. "You could have been scouting Eagle Rock for a place to live. I could have been wrapping up my job in LA. Which I did, as soon as my sister dropped Lyla on me."

"Will Lyla have any problem calling you Mommy?"

"I don't think so. I've already started wearing my hair like Rachel's and have referred to myself as what she called my sister...Mama."

Chuck nodded. "Good. Then all we need is to get her to start calling me Daddy." He swallowed hard on that word. Sarah had called him Daddy. No child had called him that since. "And if she can't do that, we won't worry. I've known small children to get confused and call their parents by their first names."

"How will you bring us into town?" Kate asked.

Chuck thought for a moment. "You're safe in Hank's

24

house for tonight. I'll go back to my bed and breakfast for the night. Once I find suitable lodging for *our family*, I'll come get you and bring you in like you're coming in from Bozeman's airport."

Kate nodded. "Sounds good. Let's talk with Hank."

Chuck glanced once more at Lyla. "She should sleep the rest of the night. But she's probably missing her mother. You might consider sleeping with her for the night."

Kate nodded. "I will. Poor thing. I know how she feels. I miss her mother, too."

Chuck held the door for Kate and half-closed it before following her down the hallway back to the living area.

He wasn't sure what he was getting himself into, or how long the assignment would last, but somehow, he had to keep his distance from the woman and child or risk breaking his heart all over again.

CHAPTER 3

K<small>ATE</small> <small>SLEPT</small> that night with Lyla snuggled up against her. She couldn't believe how much a little girl could move in her sleep. At times, she lay sideways with her feet pressed into Kate's belly. At other times, she slept with her arm around Kate's neck, her face buried against Kate's cheek.

The sweet smell of baby shampoo etched itself into Kate's memory. She'd pulled Lyla up against her and draped her arm over the child's middle. Her heart swelled and warmed to her sister's baby girl.

While she'd been busy building her career, she'd been missing the beauty of caring for such a wonderful little human being.

Sleep was slow in coming and greatly interrupted, but she couldn't be upset. Lyla hadn't asked to be caught up in whatever intrigue Rachel was up against. She hadn't asked to be dumped into the inexperienced arms of her Aunt Kate. She had suffered enough. Kate accepted the responsibility of taking care of the little girl for as long as Rachel needed. That's what family did.

Lyla settled into a deep sleep in the wee hours of the morning.

Kate finally slept as well. She woke before Lyla just as the sun was rising and edging around the curtains covering the windows.

Wanting to get a head start on the day, Kate rose, dressed in the adjoining bathroom and brushed her hair.

By the time she reentered the bedroom, Lyla was sitting up in the bed, yawning.

Kate gathered her into her arms like Chuck had suggested. "Come to Mama," she said. She carried Lyla to the bathroom to relieve herself, wash her hands and brush her hair.

Once they were finished, she took Lyla's hand. "Ready to find something to eat?"

Lyla nodded. "I'm hungry."

Together, they walked into the living room. One easily trusting little girl, and one adult scrambling to figure out the ins and outs of parenting.

Sadie stood in front of a massive fireplace with Emma playing at her feet. "Oh, good. You're awake." She lifted Emma into her arms. "Hank told me to wake you by now. He was able to find you and Chuck a cottage just on the edge of our little town of Eagle Rock."

A trickle of excitement and anticipation rippled through Kate, even while the thought of seeing Chuck again disturbed her. "That's good news."

"He contacted Chuck and let him know. Chuck will be here in thirty minutes to collect you two. I've been busy gathering items you might need for the cabin." She waved to several boxes laid out across the floor. "You'll need linens, kitchen utensils, towels and so much more. I tried to think of as much as I could. Anything else you might need, just give us a call, I probably have something. No use going out and buying all new stuff."

Bemused, Kate shook her head. "I could have purchased all of that."

Sadie smiled. "That would have defeated the purpose of looking like you're joining Chuck with things from your previous home. I have a couple of outfits I picked up in LA for when Emma gets older. They might fit Lyla now."

"I couldn't possibly take Emma's clothes."

Sadie waved her hand. "Please. Lyla needs to have something to change into. She can't show up in town in her pajamas. I'm due back in LA in a few weeks. I'll pick out more clothes for Emma. She usually goes with me."

"Are you still acting?" Kate asked.

Sadie laughed. "I am. I have gone longer between films, but I'm still showing up on the big screen."

Kate shook her head. "I don't know how you do it. Juggling a career and a baby daughter. How do working mothers manage?"

"We find good caregivers and *make* time to be with our children." Sadie grinned. "I have a fabulous nanny in LA. She's happy to work when I'm there. She keeps Emma at the studio so that I can see her on my breaks.

Fortunately, I can pay her well enough that she doesn't have to work when I'm not there."

Kate didn't say it, but Sadie implied that she understood not all working moms could afford to pay a nanny.

"Let me get those outfits. If they fit, you can keep them."

"I can afford to pay you for them," Kate offered.

"I wouldn't let you. They're my gift to Lyla. Poor little thing has to be feeling the stress of all the changes in her life." Sadie held out Emma. "Do you mind holding her for a moment?"

Before Kate could beg off, Emma leaned toward her.

Kate had to take her, or the baby would have fallen.

Emma wrapped her arms around Kate's neck and gave her a wet baby kiss.

Instead of being repulsed by the baby spittle, Kate laughed. "Is she always this good with strangers?"

"Not everyone. She seems to be a good judge of character." Sadie grinned and hurried from the room.

While Kate held Emma, Lyla found a basket full of brightly colored toys. She pulled out one toy at a time until the basket was empty.

Emma batted at Kate's gold hoop earrings, determined to capture one and put it into her mouth.

Kate held onto the squirming baby, afraid she'd drop the child. She kept a close eye on Lyla to make sure she didn't get too close to the fireplace or stick her fingers into a light socket. She'd heard that little kids did things like that.

Emma grabbed both of her ears and deposited a kiss on Kate's cheek.

"Thank you, Kate." Sadie emerged from the hallway, carrying a stack of little girls clothing. "I'll take Emma." She laid the stack of clothes on the back of the sofa and relieved Kate of her burden.

Kate glanced through the outfits on the back of the sofa and held them up to Lyla's back, one at a time.

The child played on with the toys she'd found, oblivious to her aunt.

"All three of these outfits should fit," Kate declared. "Thank you."

"You're more than welcome." Sadie glanced out the front window. "Looks like your bodyguard has arrived. We can load the boxes into the back of his truck."

Kate's heartbeat sped. A cautious look out the window made it beat even faster.

Chuck dropped down from his truck and strode toward the house. Tall, broad-shouldered and rugged, the man had swagger and probably didn't know it. Even the graying at his temples only added to his attractiveness.

Heat coiled in Kate's core. She hadn't been that aroused by a man in a very long time. And this guy wasn't a spring chicken. Perhaps that's what she liked most about him. He was mature, confident in his skin and exuded pure masculinity out of every pore of his body.

Sadie met him at the door. "Come on in, Chuck. We were just about to start breakfast. You can join us."

His gaze scanned the room, slowing as it passed Kate. "Where's Hank?"

"He's been up for hours, working on some background checks for one of the other new agents. He'll join us once I get the bacon cooking." Sadie winked. "The man likes bacon. I'm sure it'll harden his arteries, but he reminds me all the time that life's too short to skip the bacon."

"I couldn't agree with him more." He nodded toward Kate. "But I thought we'd hit the diner in town. We might as well establish our cover right away."

"Oh." Kate twisted her fingers into the hem of her shirt. She'd thought she'd have a little more time before she was alone with Chuck. Time to adjust to the thought of pretending to be his wife, acting like a loving couple with a daughter. "Okay. I can be ready in just a few minutes." She shot a glance toward Lyla.

"I'll watch her," Chuck said. He held out his hands. "How's my little girl this morning?"

Lyla lifted her arms, still holding the stuffed unicorn she'd picked out of the box.

Chuck lifted her up and settled her into the crook of his arm. He leaned in and gave her a noisy, smacking kiss on the cheek.

Lyla laughed and kissed him back with just as much bravado. Then she hugged him tightly around the neck.

Kate shook her head. She never got that kind of reaction from Lyla, and she was blood-related. The man had the child completely charmed.

And he was charming Kate in the process. "How do you do that?"

Chuck stared across at Kate, his lips still curved in a smile. "Do what?"

Charm the fool out of me, she wanted to say, but clamped her lips tight to keep from telling him exactly how confused he made her feel. "Nothing. I'll be right back." She spun on her heel, grabbed the clothes Sadie had given Lyla and ran into the bedroom, closing the door behind her.

Kate stood with her back to the door, pressing her hands to her heated cheeks. How *did* he do that? With only a smile, he turned her knees to mush. And the way he was so at ease with Lyla melted Kate's heart like nothing she'd ever experienced.

She straightened and pushed back her shoulders. Kate hadn't taken an indefinite leave of absence from her work to flirt with Lyla's bodyguard. The sooner she got that through her head, the better. Having Chuck pretend to be her husband and the father of her child was a temporary arrangement, necessary to protect Lyla. Once the threat was vanquished, Kate would head back to LA, Lyla would return to Rachel and her husband, and Chuck would move on to his next assignment.

Don't get personal with the hired help, she schooled herself.

In short order, she packed her toiletries and Lyla's new clothes into her suitcase, zipped it and set it on the floor. Then she gathered Lyla's blanket and Sid, reminded again of how little she had.

Her thoughts returned to her sister, and her heart ached. What had Rachel gotten herself into? Where was

Myles? How could he let anything happen to his family? What kind of man let his wife ditch their baby and run?

Unless he hadn't known Rachel would run away from him and take their child. In which case, was she running because Myles was abusive?

Kate wished Rachel was there. She had a hundred questions for her. The only thing she knew was that her twin was in trouble. When she was sure Lyla was safe, she'd work on finding Rachel and helping her through whatever trouble she was up against.

With the blanket under one arm, Kate wheeled the suitcase out of the bedroom and down the hallway to the living room.

Chuck sat on the floor, pulling Lyla's hair up into a ponytail.

Lyla had been changed into colorful knit pants and a shirt with polka dots and ruffles.

"I found another outfit for Lyla," Sadie said with a smile as she handed Chuck an elastic band. "And we thought Lyla might like her hair up and out of her face." Sadie motioned toward the window. "It's pretty windy outside today."

The man handled the child's baby-fine hair like a pro, appearing at ease despite how incongruous the big man looked next to the little girl.

When he finished, he rose to his feet, lifted Lyla into his arms, and nodded. "Ready?"

No, she wasn't. Not when it meant being alone with this man who ignited flames in Kate when she'd thought herself flame-resistant. "Yes." Given she'd more or less begged him to take the job, she couldn't balk now. He was the only man she knew, or felt she could trust, to take care of her and Lyla until they figured out what to do next. "Let's go."

Chuck led the way through the door, pausing long enough to scan the area before holding the door wide for Kate.

Sadie, holding Emma on her hip, exited as well and stood on the porch. "We're so glad you came to us, Kate." She smiled. "Don't worry. Chuck's an amazing man. He had to be to make it into the Navy SEALs." Sadie hugged Kate. Emma giggled and grabbed Kate's hair in her fist.

Kate laughed, unclenched the child's hand from her hair and kissed her little fist. "Thank you for helping and for all the things you've given us."

"Maybe we can set up a play date for the girls," Sadie suggested.

A play date. Sure, she'd heard of them, but she wasn't sure she was comfortable with the idea. "Uh, that would be nice. I guess."

"Let us assess the situation first," Hank said from behind Sadie.

The former SEAL curled his arm around his wife's waist and dropped a kiss on top of Emma's head. "Let us know if you need anything. The cottage is right on the edge of Eagle Rock on a less traveled road. Only people with a reason to go down that road should be going down that road."

Chuck nodded and held out his hand to Hank. "Thanks. I'll keep a close watch over these two."

"I know you will." Hank clasped his hand. "I knew

you were the right man for the job. You need anything, just give me a yell."

Chuck led the way off the porch and to the passenger side of his pickup. "Do you have a car?"

Kate shook her head. "No. Hank picked me up at the airport. I didn't want to risk driving cross-country with Lyla. Not when I might have a tail following me."

"Good thinking. Though, if someone wanted to find you badly enough, they'd follow your credit card purchases."

Kate frowned. "To move fast, I had to use what I had."

Chuck settled Lyla into the back seat and adjusted the seat belt to fit as snugly as possible across her little lap. "After we meet the realtor at the cottage, we need to find a place to purchase a child's car seat."

"Definitely," Kate agreed. "And we need to stock the pantry with food. I'm not sure how long we'll be at this."

"Hank said the cottage came furnished." Chuck moved out, closed the back door and turned to hold the front passenger door for Kate. "That will be one less expense you'll have to incur."

"How big is the cottage?" Kate asked.

"I have no idea. We'll find out when we get there."

That was what Kate was afraid of. Any small cottage would be all the smaller with Chuck inside. His broad shoulders filled even the largest of rooms.

And if it had only a single bedroom? Where would they all sleep? That same trickle of excitement rippled through her center. All because of one tall, well-muscled Navy SEAL who would be Lyla's bodyguard and pretend daddy for however long it took for Rachel to return for her daughter.

And what if Rachel didn't come back?

Kate's breath lodged in her throat. Being twins, she'd always felt an awareness of her sister. Surely, she'd know if something awful happened. But then she hadn't known her sister was in distress. If she had, she would have offered to help in any way possible.

Yet, it had been Rachel who'd reached out in her time of need.

Kate hated that she'd been such a terrible sister she hadn't known Rachel was in trouble. Hell, she hadn't seen Rachel since she'd moved to Idaho over three years before. Sure, they'd talked on the phone, but Kate had always been in a hurry to end the call and get on with whatever project she'd been working. And she hadn't met Lyla, until the child had landed on her doorstep.

Her heart hurt at her failure as a sister.

What was important now was to take care of Rachel's daughter and then find Rachel.

WHEN CHUCK HELD Lyla in his arms, all the feelings he'd felt for Sarah came flooding back. No matter that it had been years since he'd held his daughter, the same emotions were still there. With Maya, he'd had the advantage of her growing on him from an infant to a healthy one-year-old. She'd sneaked into his life one day at a time. But Lyla was about the same size, if a year older, than Sarah had been when she'd been killed in a car wreck.

Sarah had had blond hair and smelled of baby shampoo, just like Lyla.

His chest constricted, making it difficult to breathe. He forced air into his lungs and marched on, like he always did, reminding himself this was a job. Once the situation resolved, he'd be on to the next assignment. Kate and Lyla would be gone from Montana.

Don't get attached.

He glanced toward Kate.

She was a pretty woman with blond hair and blue eyes, much like Lyla. He could imagine her twin looking exactly like her and how much trouble they must have caused growing up.

He thought it strange that she didn't have the slightest clue how to be a mother. What happened to good old maternal instinct? Kate seemed so awkward around her niece.

"Are you sure you're Lyla's aunt?" Chuck asked as he slid into the driver's seat.

"I'm pretty sure. All I've had from my sister was an occasional photograph of Lyla. But there's no mistaking her features. She looks just like we did at her age. But if you're concerned I might have kidnapped the child, why don't you take us straight to the sheriff's office? I probably should have started there in the first place. My sister begged me not to take the situation to the police, or I would have." She stared out the window. "Do you know where we're going?"

"Not hardly," he muttered, shaking his head. "I have the address. It can't be too hard to find. Eagle Rock isn't a large community."

They accomplished the drive into town in silence. Kate glanced all around, keeping an eye on the road ahead and behind them. After what happened at her apartment in LA, Kate wasn't sure about anything. The man who'd broken down her door had meant business. Thankfully, the cops had arrived in time to help.

Following Hank's directions, Chuck drove through the quaint little town of Eagle Rock with its one main street, several side streets, a medical clinic, sheriff's office, tavern and diner.

Kate stared out the window eagerly, wanting to know whatever she could about the little Montana town she'd be spending the next couple of days in while hiding out.

ON THE OTHER side of town, Chuck slowed and glanced down at the directions on his cellphone. He turned left onto a short road that ended in a field of green hay.

Two houses lined one side of the road. One was white with blue shutters. The other, the one they were renting, was yellow with white shutters.

The houses were separated by a dingy white picket fence in need of fresh paint, and a row of pink, climbing, tea roses that softened its appearance and made it appear quaint rather than neglected. Chuck rolled down his window and inhaled the lush, rich scent of roses and freshly cut grass. Apparently, the yard had recently been mowed and smelled like spring.

Having lived in apartments when he wasn't deployed, Chuck couldn't help but feel a connection to this little cottage on the quiet little road. Yes, it could stand a fresh paint job, and the bushes needed trimming, but the yellow and white combination reminded him of daisies and sunshine.

If he, Lyla and Kate were a real family, this was the kind of place he'd want to come home to.

Chuck pulled into the driveway and turned off the truck engine. "Let's check it out for a few minutes, make a list of what we need, and get to the diner for that breakfast I promised."

Kate nodded and pushed open her door before Chuck could jump down and hurry around to her side. He chuckled softly. Apparently, she was used to opening her own doors.

Which was just as well because, whenever he was close to Kate, he struggled for words and his libido reminded him of how long it had been since he'd been with a woman.

He had to remind himself that his reaction to Kate was purely chemical. Nothing he could stop. But he'd have to minimize its effects to avoid any complications in their relationship. Kate and Lyla were a job, nothing more.

He opened the back door to the truck, unbuckled Lyla's seat belt and set her on her feet in the grass.

She shot off like a rocket toward the house. "It's yellow. Our new house is yellow," she cried. She was up on the porch and swinging on the porch swing before Kate or Chuck could warn her to wait until they checked it out.

Kate smiled. "She likes the color. Rachel also likes yellow."

Chuck stared at Kate, amazed at the transformation a simple smile could make to a woman's face. For a moment, the worry and heartache were gone. In that fleeting moment, Chuck could see how beautiful Kate was.

Then the shadows returned, and Kate looked at Chuck. "I hope Rachel is all right."

"I do too." He shifted his gaze to Lyla, swinging on the porch. "A child needs her mother."

"What if Rachel doesn't come back?" Kate touched his arm. "What if something awful has happened to her?"

He covered her hand with his. "My mama always told me, *Don't borrow trouble.*" Chuck gave her hand a comforting squeeze. "Take one day at a time. I'm sure Hank's working on finding your sister." He nodded toward the house. "Let's get moved in and start looking like a family." Drawing her hand through the crook of his elbow, he led her to the front door. If anyone was watching through a window, they'd see a man, his wife and their small daughter.

All the way across the yard to the front door, Chuck used his SEAL skills of situational awareness, scanning the area for potential threats. No matter how good it felt to have a beautiful woman on his arm, or to hold a child in his arms, he had to maintain his focus. These two people were only his to protect, not to fall in love with.

CHAPTER 4

KATE HELD tight to Lyla's hand as she brushed past Chuck and stepped through the door.

The interior of the house was perhaps as quaint as the exterior. The rooms had been freshly painted and smelled like new.

Fortunately, the house came furnished, so they wouldn't have to invest in couches, beds and other items. What was there appeared to be rather dated, but lovingly cared for. A floral-print, overstuffed couch and a lounge chair in a coordinating, solid burgundy graced the original hardwood living room floor and faced what appeared to be a working fireplace. The coffee table probably dated back to the late 1960s with dainty crocheted doilies spread across the surface.

Paintings on the wall depicted snow-covered mountains and fields of wildflowers. A picture window looked out over a backyard of lush, green grass and rose bushes planted along the fence line.

"This is really cute," Kate commented. She strolled through the living room into the kitchen where a retro table stood with a Formica top and metal legs. The chairs were covered in bright-red, shiny fabric.

"I feel like I stepped into the past on the set for one of those family shows from the fifties," Chuck said.

"I know. But I like it. It makes me think of a simpler time." Kate studied the antique gas stove and the deep, white, porcelain sink. "I bet there's a clawfoot tub in the bathroom." She hurried to the only bathroom in the three-bedroom house to find what she knew would be there. "Ha! See?" She stood back and let Chuck lean into the bathroom.

A huge old clawfoot tub stood against the wall with a shower curtain hung on a circular rod above.

Lyla ducked between their legs and ran to the tub. "Can I have a bath?"

Chuck laughed. "If we'd had a tub like that when I was a kid, I would have loved taking a bath." He patted Lyla's head. "Later, darlin', we have to unload stuff from the truck and go get some breakfast."

Kate's stomach rumbled, reminding her that she hadn't eaten since the night before.

Chuck left them in the hallway and made a quick inspection of the rooms and closets, probably looking for bogeymen hiding out there.

Kate did her own appraisal. The house had three bedrooms. Two of them were set up with beds. One had been used as an office with a large desk and office chair, no bed. The smaller bedroom had a twin bed and a matching dresser. The master bedroom wasn't very large but had a queen-sized bed in the middle of the room and a long, low dresser with a mirror. The bed was made up with a blue and white comforter. White, lacey curtains hung in the windows. Two beds, two adults and one child. If Kate and Chuck were really married, the bed situation would work.

But they weren't, and it wouldn't. Kate stared at the bed that would fit a husband and wife, and her pulse beat faster. Her imagination took flight. She could picture lying in that bed with Chuck. He'd take up most of the space with his broad shoulders and long body. It would mean sleeping up against his hard muscles, pressed close to keep from falling off the bed. What woman would complain?

"We'll need to run by the hardware store for a dead-bolt lock and a few replacement locks for the windows." Chuck's voice jerked Kate back to reality.

"We can do that," Kate said. She spun away from the master bedroom and forced a smile to her face while her heart pounded against her ribs.

"I'll unload the boxes, then we can leave."

"I can help," Kate offered, following him to the door.

"Just keep an eye on Lyla." He nodded toward the toddler peering through the picture window into the backyard. "It won't take me long. There isn't much."

"Can I go outside to play?" Lyla asked.

"Not yet, sweetie," Kate said. She went to stand beside Lyla and stared out into a yard that would be the perfect size for a swing set.

Lyla reached up and slipped her little hand into Kate's. "I'm hungry."

"We'll go to the diner in just a few minutes." She knelt on the floor. "Do you think you'll like living here with Mama and Daddy?" Kate figured she'd better start training Lyla to call her and Chuck by their pretend titles. The sooner she did, the better their cover would be.

Lyla tilted her head. "Yes. It's pretty." She ran to the couch, pulled herself up onto the cushions and patted the space beside her. "Come. Sit down. It's soft, too."

Kate sat beside the little girl and smiled. "You're right. It's very soft and comfortable."

Chuck carried in the boxes Sadie had sent and laid them on the floor in the front entryway.

"Daddy," Kate called out, making it a point to call Chuck Daddy. "Sadie said there was a doll in one of those boxes. I don't suppose you see it, do you? Lyla might like to take it with her to the diner."

Chuck stopped halfway through the front door, his eyes widening. For a moment, he remained as if frozen in time. Then he drew in a deep breath and entered, set down the box he'd been carrying, and dug into the one beside it. A moment later, he held up a soft doll with a ruffled dress and bright, blond hair. "Is this what you were looking for?"

Lyla squealed and launched herself off the couch. She ran toward Chuck with her arms reaching out for the doll.

He held it out of her reach. "What do you say?"

She stopped and stood as straight as an arrow and said, "Please, may I have it?"

Chuck dropped to one knee and handed her the doll. "Yes, you may."

"Say thank you, Daddy," Kate prompted.

Chuck remained kneeling in front of Lyla.

"Thank you, Daddy," Lyla said and clutched the doll to her chest. "She's beautiful. I'm going to call her Sarah."

Chuck's jaw tightened, and he closed his eyes as if he was in pain. Then he pushed to his feet and left the house.

If she hadn't witnessed his reaction to Lyla, she might have missed the fact Chuck was affected by the little girl's words. What had upset the former SEAL? That she'd called him Daddy? Or that she'd named the doll Sarah?

He was back a few seconds later with the last box. Once he set it on the floor, he stood straight. "Are you two ready for breakfast?"

"Yes!' Lyla ran toward the door.

Chuck scooped her up into his arms and waited for Kate to join them. Then he walked with them out to the truck and helped them inside.

Kate liked that he took the time to adjust the seat belt across Lyla's lap and worried that she didn't have a car seat. He cared about the child who wasn't even his. She imagined he'd be the same with his own children. At his age, he should have had a family of his own. Kate wondered why such a good-looking guy was still single. Not that she was in the market, but she was curious about the man who was pretending to be her husband.

Perhaps that evening, she'd ask him a few questions

and get to know him better. It would help to make their pretense more believable. At least, that's how she'd pose the questions. It wouldn't hurt to get to know the man better.

On a professional level, not a personal level, of course.

She studied him out of the corner of her eye as he slid into the seat beside her. Yeah, a purely professional level. Getting personal would be dangerous.

CHUCK DROVE the few short blocks to the only diner in town. He'd been there a couple of times, by himself and with other members of the Brotherhood Protectors. The food was good, and he didn't have to cook it.

His chest still hurt from what Lyla had said. First, she'd called him Daddy. Then she'd named her doll Sarah. Where she'd heard that name was a mystery. But it hit him square in the heart. Sarah had been her daddy's girl. She could do no wrong in his eyes and he would give his life to have her back. But that could never be. She'd died years ago, and he thought he'd gotten over it.

But he knew it was all a joke to think you ever got over losing a child. He never wanted to forget her, and why would he? The memories he had were good ones. He held onto them because he'd loved Sarah with all his heart.

He pulled up in front of Al's Diner, mentally pulling himself together. Now wasn't the time to stroll down memory lane or start feeling the heartache of loss all over again.

When he shifted into park, he opened his door and dropped down out of the truck. By the time he rounded the hood, Kate had already climbed out and was unhooking Lyla's seat belt.

"You've got to let me open doors for you," Chuck said softly enough only Kate could hear.

"Why?" she asked and lifted Lyla out of the truck and into her arms.

"Because that's what husbands do for their wives."

She stared at him as if he'd grown a horn. "Really? In this day and age?"

Chuck ground his teeth together. "My mama taught me to treat ladies with care and respect. Opening doors is a part of that."

Kate's eyes narrowed. "Just how old are you? Ninety-three?"

A frown pulled Chuck's brows together. "I might be older than you, but I have a lot of life left in me."

"I'm sure you do." Kate's mouth curved into a smile. "Better get all that living in while you can. Your days are numbered." Then she winked. "You know I'm yanking your chain, don't you?"

He shook his head. "I believe you say exactly what you mean."

When she turned with Lyla in her arms, he smacked her ass.

"Hey," Kate spun around and glared at him.

"What?" He held up his hands. "I'm just doing what a husband would do with his wife. Good job acting like you're offended." He gripped her arm and pulled her up against his chest. "Now, kiss me and look like we're making up."

He bent his head and captured her mouth with his.

She didn't have time to protest, and he liked that he'd caught her off guard.

When he stepped away, he moved back far enough she couldn't slap the smile off his face.

She raised her hand, all right, but not to slap him. Instead, she stared at him, pressing her fingers to her kiss-swollen lips.

When Chuck was sure Kate wouldn't slap him, he leaned close to Lyla's ear. "How's my sweet little girl? Want a kiss, too?"

"Yes, please," she said and presented her cheek for him.

He bent close to land a noisy smack on Lyla's petal-soft face.

She giggled and raised her shoulders. "That tickles."

"Oh, yeah?" Chuck blew a raspberry on her neck.

Lyla squealed and giggled again.

Chuck glanced over the top of the child's head. "Now, we look like a family." He held out his elbow.

Kate hooked her arm through his and walked with him to the entrance.

As soon as they entered the diner, a man wearing an apron stepped out of the kitchen. "Have a seat, your waitress will be with you in a minute." He pushed through the swinging door into the kitchen, yelling, "Daisy! Need you out front."

"Coming!" a feminine voice called out. A blond-haired, blue-eyed waitress backed through the swinging door, carrying a huge tray laden with plates of food. "Grab a seat anywhere. I'll be right with you."

Chuck steered Kate and Lyla to a booth in the back corner of the diner. He guided them onto one of the bench seats and took the other, facing the entrance.

A few moments later, Daisy plopped laminated menus in front of them. "Good morning," she said with a big smile. "I'm Daisy. I'll be your server. What can I get you to drink?"

Chuck chose coffee, Kate chose hot tea and asked for a cup of milk for Lyla.

"Got it," Daisy said. "Be right back."

The pretty, young woman practically sprinted back to the kitchen. Moments later, she appeared with the glasses balanced on a large tray.

Once she'd set down their cups and glasses, she pulled out a pad and pen. "What melts your butter today?" she asked.

Kate ordered a yogurt and a cup of fruit.

Chuck ordered two eggs over easy and toast.

Kate leaned toward Lyla. "Would you like eggs or cereal?"

"Cereal, please," Lyla said. "The kind with the marshmallows."

"Cereal, it is—with the marshmallows," the waitress said with a smile. She pocketed her pen and reached for the large tray. When she had it perched at her shoulder, she grinned. "You're new in town, aren't you?"

Kate returned her smile. "We are."

"Are you visiting or staying?" Daisy asked.

"We're thinking about staying," Chuck responded. "We're renting a place now but will be looking around to buy."

"Looking for a house in town? Or a piece of property a little farther out?"

"In town," Chuck said.

"A little farther out," Kate said at the same time.

Chuck laughed. "We haven't decided. Since we're new around here, we'll leave the decision open until we've seen a few places."

"Out in the country gives the little ones a place to run wild, but in town they can go to the park and play with other children." Daisy shrugged. "It's whatever you prefer. People around here make it happen."

"What about you," Kate asked. "Did you grow up in Eagle Rock?"

Daisy nodded. "Yes, ma'am. But a lot of my friends lived out of town. I visited some of the ranches around here and learned to fish, hunt and ride horses. So, I guess I didn't miss much."

"Eagle Rock is pretty small," Kate remarked. "What keeps people from leaving?"

Daisy shifted the tray at her shoulder. "Many of the young people leave. Some go into the military, and then come back later. Me...I'm limited by money. Soon as I get enough, I'm off to college."

Kate nodded. "Good for you. Even if you come back to Eagle Rock, you'll come back with more than you left with."

"That's what I figure. But I plan to learn a lot and see the world before I come back."

"Admirable aspirations," Kate concurred.

"Well, I'd better get back to it. We're shorthanded today." Daisy rushed back to the kitchen with their order and emerged with another tray loaded with food. She delivered the food to a large family at a set of tables and refilled their glasses. A few minutes later, she appeared at their table again, this time with their food.

She set the plates in front of them. "Anything else I can get you?"

"No, thank you," Chuck replied. Though Daisy was nice, she was standing in the way of him studying every person in the diner.

Once the waitress left them, Chuck lifted his fork, stabbed the fried eggs and a piece of toast and brought it to his lips. He bit into the savory flavor and glanced around the diner, studying every face, committing them to memory.

The family at a table on the other side of the diner had the typical mother and father. What wasn't typical was the fact they were accompanied by a cool eight children. How their parents could afford to feed that many at a diner was beyond Chuck.

A couple of middle-aged men in jeans and jackets sat in a booth two over from the one where Chuck sat. They wore shirts with matching company logos embroidered on them. Before them on the table lay blueprints of a building.

Two gray-haired women sat at a table sipping tea, and four young men wearing reflective vests, jeans and work boots filled another booth, all drinking coffee and eating big platters of eggs and pancakes.

A young couple entered the diner with their daughter who appeared to be a couple years older than Lyla.

"Find a seat. I'll be right with you," Daisy called out.

Daisy topped off Chuck's coffee before she moved on to the newer customers.

"See anyone who looks like they could give us a headache?" Kate whispered.

"No," Chuck said, but he wasn't letting down his guard.

"Should I make a list of the groceries we need?" Kate asked. "I don't know what kind of meals you like to eat."

"I eat anything I don't have to cook."

Kate chuckled. "That narrows it down."

"I don't expect you to do all the cooking." Chuck lifted his chin. "I can cook a handful of meals. Nothing fancy. Chili, spaghetti, grilled anything and eggs."

"Good. Between the two of us, we won't starve or resort to eating out every meal." Kate twisted her lips into a wry grin. "At the grocery store, you can pick your ingredients, and I'll pick mine. I have a limited repertoire. I can make a mean lasagna, gumbo, pot roast and chicken salad."

Chuck nodded. "Point is not to get wrapped up in meal prep. Whatever is easy is fine with me. We can buy lunch meat and hot dogs, and I'll be fine."

"You're on." Kate finished her yogurt and fruit.

Lyla played with her doll, forgetting to eat her cereal.

"Lyla, sweetie, finish your cereal so we can get back to the cottage and you can play with Sarah."

Chuck winced. How could he tell a little girl she couldn't name her doll Sarah? Hell, he couldn't. Lyla had every right to name the doll anything she wanted. Just because it made a grown man want to cry every time he heard the name wasn't reason enough to force a three-year-old to change the doll's name.

He glanced up and caught Kate's gaze. His eyes narrowed. Had she seen him wince? Vowing to do a better job of hiding his emotions, Chuck shuttered his eyes and dug out his wallet. He tossed bills onto the table, enough to cover their meals, and stood. "Ready?"

Kate turned to Lyla. "Did you eat enough?"

"Yes," Lyla rubbed her tummy. "I'm full."

They left the diner and headed for the hardware store first.

There, Chuck purchased deadbolt locks for the front and rear doors. He bought replacement locks for the windows that needed them. He also picked up a couple of security devices to attach to the windows and doors that made piercing noises when set off. They weren't a real security system that connected with the sheriff's department, but they might scare off a would-be intruder.

While he hurried down the aisles of the hardware store, he made Kate and Lyla stand at the end of each aisle he was on. That way he could keep an eye on them. Others might have laughed. What could possibly happen in a hardware store?

While he found hardware, Kate found a pair of denim overalls in Lyla's size, a pink blouse and a pint-sized pair of cowboy boots to fit her as well.

Chuck insisted on paying for the purchases. He didn't want Kate's credit cards to show up in Eagle Rock and alert anyone who might be tracking her.

Chuck wasn't taking any chances. No one was looking for him, so using his cards posed no threat. He just had to keep Kate from alerting anyone to her whereabouts until her sister could be found and the situation resolved.

CHAPTER 5

KATE DIDN'T LIKE IT, but it made sense for Chuck to pay for their purchases. When she could, she'd pay him back any money he spent on them. She had employed *him.* He shouldn't have to pay for anything. Hopefully, he'd put all his receipts on an expense report, to be paid when the situation was resolved.

Kate couldn't believe how everything seemed to be upside down in her life. From a neat, orderly existence to utter chaos. For now, all she could do was go with the flow.

She sat back in her seat and stared at the road ahead as Chuck drove them to the grocery store.

Once inside, Kate said, "Lyla's getting tired. We can cover more ground if we split up. I'll take Lyla with me. You get the juice, milk, eggs and cheese. I'll find the meats, cereal and spices."

Chuck hesitated for a moment, his gaze moving around the store's interior.

"Look, the store isn't that big. We won't be out of yelling distance if anything should happen," Kate insisted.

He sighed. "Okay. But I'll make it fast and join you as soon as I have my items."

"Deal." Kate took one of the shopping carts and lifted Lyla to sit in it.

After a few minutes, Kate had selected the items on her list—hamburger for Chuck's chili and cereal with marshmallows for Lyla's breakfast. When she rolled down the candy aisle, Kate paused in front of the nuts and raisins.

Lyla pulled her legs out of the holes in the cart and stood up.

"Lyla, sit down," Kate admonished. She tried to get Lyla to take her seat again, but the child was having none of it.

"I want candy," Lyla said. "Please."

"No, sweetie. Candy is bad for your teeth and will make your tummy hurt."

"I want candy," she said, her voice rising. She leaned out of the cart.

If Kate hadn't grabbed her, she would have fallen to the floor. Once Kate had her in her arms, she struggled to hold onto the squirming child.

"Lyla, please. I can't hold you when you wiggle so much."

"Want down."

Kate set her on her feet. Before she could grab her hand, Lyla snatched a package of candy and darted away.

Kate lunged for her but missed.

Lyla disappeared around the end of the aisle with Kate chasing after her.

"Lyla!" Kate called out. "Chuck!" She needed help. One three-year-old couldn't be so fast she could get away that quickly, but she had.

Kate cleared the end of the aisles but didn't see Lyla anywhere.

Chuck burst from a couple aisles over. "What's wrong?"

"Lyla got away from me." Kate didn't wait for him to catch up to her. She swung right and ran past the next aisle. Lyla wasn't in that one either.

Kate kept going. When she rounded the end of the one, she spotted a flash of blond hair.

Kate ran to where Lyla stood in front of another little girl and her parents. "Lyla, sweetie, you scared me."

"I found a friend." Lyla pointed to the other little girl who was a little older and a foot taller.

"We wondered where her parents were," the mother said. "Hi, I'm Becca, this is my husband Daniel and my daughter Mary." She held out her hand. "We're new in town."

Kate let go of the breath she'd been holding since Lyla ran off. "Thank goodness she didn't get far." Kate took the hand the woman extended and shook. "Thank you for being here to stop her. I'm Kate and this is Chuck, my...husband and my...daughter, Lyla."

"You have no idea how glad I am to meet someone else with a child," Becca said. "I was afraid Mary would get lonely here. I haven't seen a whole lot of children."

"Me either," Kate admitted. "Please, don't let us keep you. I don't know what got into Lyla to make her run off like that."

"Three can be a difficult age." Becca smiled down at Lyla. "Some children like to think they're independent. They can be stubborn or unruly. Sometimes it just takes a firm hand and structure to guide them," Becca said. "Mary's terrible twos lasted until she was almost four."

Kate's eyes narrowed. "I don't remember telling you my daughter was three."

Becca's eyebrows rose. "No? Well, I guessed based on her size and vocabulary."

The woman's explanation wasn't great, but it was plausible. Kate turned to Becca's child. "How old are you, Mary?"

At first the little girl didn't answer.

Becca gave her a nudge. "Tell Miss Kate how old you are."

The little girl had dark braids and big, brown eyes. She turned those eyes up to Kate and held up her hand with all her fingers extended. "I'm five."

"Nice to meet you, Mary," Kate said. "We hope to see you around town." She glanced back at Chuck.

He moved forward and extended his hand to Becca. "Nice to meet you." Then he held out his hand to Daniel. The two men shook hands and exchanged nods.

"If you'll excuse us, we need to get going," Chuck said. He lifted Lyla into his arms, removed the package of candy from her fingers and stared into her face. "No candy," he said firmly. "You can have a banana when we get back to the house."

Lyla puckered up as if to start crying. "But, I want—"

Chuck shook his head once. "No."

Lyla sniffed, her eyes wide, but she didn't argue. Instead, she laid her head on Chuck's shoulder and wrapped her arm around his neck.

"It was nice to meet you," Kate repeated to Becca. And she hurried off to find her cart and Chuck's. A few minutes later, they'd purchased their groceries and loaded them into the truck along with a car seat they were lucky enough to find for Lyla. When Chuck buckled her in this time, Kate felt a lot better about the child's safety.

Once they were all settled into the truck, Kate leaned back against the seat and let go of a long breath. "I never knew how hard it was to raise a child. I think I lost a year off my life with the scare she gave me."

A chuckle rumbled beside her. "You'll get used to it. Most children come as infants. That gives you the time you need to adjust as they grow."

Kate turned to Chuck. "Why are you so good with Lyla?" Then a thought occurred to her and her face heated. "Oh my God. You're married, aren't you? And you must have children of your own." Holy crud, she'd been lusting after a married man.

Chuck's jaw tightened, and he got that same look he'd had when Lyla had named her doll Sarah. He looked as if he was in pain.

Kate held up her hand. "I'm sorry. It's none of my business. Forget I said anything. This is all just a job. You don't owe me any information about you and your life outside the Brotherhood Protectors."

A minute passed, stretching into two as he navigated the streets of Eagle Rock. He didn't say anything, and Kate had decided to forget she'd asked.

It wasn't until they'd carried all the groceries into the house and closed the door behind them that Chuck spoke. "I'm not married," he said.

A rush of relief washed over her, making her lips curl upward. She stopped short of saying *Thank God.*

"I was married many years ago. And I had a daughter."

He'd *had* a daughter. Kate shot a quick glance his way. His gray eyes seemed darker, and his lips pressed tightly together. "Had?" she asked, and then wished she hadn't.

The raw pain in his gaze nearly took her breath away.

"My wife and daughter were killed in an automobile accident when our little girl was only two."

Kate's heart dropped to the pit of her belly. "I'm so sorry," she said, a sob choking her words.

"Don't worry about it. That was a long time ago."

"Maybe so, but I can't imagine anyone really gets over something like that." She touched his arm. "Was your daughter's name Sarah?"

He nodded.

Kate closed her eyes to the man's agony. "Is that why you didn't want to work with us?" She knew the answer before he responded.

"Yes."

She tipped her head and frowned. "Wow. Then why did you agree to help?"

He nodded toward Lyla who'd curled up on the floral couch with her doll named Sarah and had fallen asleep. "Because of her. I knew Hank didn't have anyone else experienced at working with children." He gave a twisted smile. "I couldn't walk away. She needed me to help look after her."

The man was breaking Kate's heart. "You must have loved your family so very much."

He nodded. "At the time, I had wished I could have died with them," he admitted. "But they were in Virginia. I was in Afghanistan on a mission. I didn't know until two days after they'd died. I flew back in time to attend the funeral."

Kate could imagine his heartache at seeing his wife and little girl lying in eternal repose in caskets. Her own heart ached for him.

"How long ago did it happen?" she asked so softly he could ignore the question if he wanted.

"Fourteen years, two months and…six days."

"And you haven't remarried," she stated.

"I couldn't. As a Navy SEAL, I couldn't do it again. I wasn't there for my wife and baby. I refused to subject another woman to that kind of responsibility and loneliness."

"Or yourself to more heartbreak," Kate concluded.

Chuck drew in a deep breath. "Now, if you'll excuse me, I have work to do to make this place a little more secure."

She stepped back. "Thank you." Kate didn't say more.

By the tightness of his jaw, Chuck had withdrawn, choosing to handle his grief in stoic silence.

He deserved to be left to his own personal space.

Kate fought the urge to wrap her arms around the big man and hold on tightly until all his pain went away. But that would be silly, and the gesture would be unwanted. They'd only just met. A big, tough guy like Chuck wouldn't appreciate sympathy or empathy. A former SEAL probably powered through everything life had to throw at him.

From her own experience, it could be lonely shouldering through life by yourself. Now that she had Lyla, Kate realized not only the level of responsibility, but also the capacity for love.

Her gaze shifted from Lyla's sleeping form to follow Chuck.

The man knew how to wear a pair of jeans. They hugged his hips like a second skin and pulled tightly across powerful thighs. His T-shirt stretched across impossibly broad shoulders, straining against thick biceps.

Rather than make him appear old, the gray hair at his temples made him look dangerously sexy.

Kate worked through the house, finding places for the groceries and cleaning supplies they'd purchased. Then she went to work making the two beds with the sheets and pillows and pillowcases Sadie had sent in the boxes. She placed towels in a neat stack in the bathroom and marveled about how the few things they'd added to the cozy cottage made it feel even more personal, like a home.

Her gaze wandered often to Chuck as he installed new deadbolt locks to the front and back doors. Making the beds with Chuck in the room working on the window latches was more exhilarating than Kate would have thought. Her heart beat fast, and her breathing became so erratic, she felt as if she'd run a marathon by the time he left the room.

If he wasn't the hired help, and she wasn't so worried about her sister, Kate might consider asking Chuck out for a drink. Maybe dinner and a nightcap.

She smoothed the sheets over the queen-sized bed and imagined what might come after the nightcap.

Kate shook her head and squared her shoulders. Her sister was missing, she had a niece to protect, and Chuck wasn't on the market for anyone. Kate had to get a grip or risk a little frustration and possible heartache of her own.

She carried her suitcase into the bedroom and pulled out a T-shirt. She might as well get comfortable and do some cleaning. Maybe it would help get her mind off the sexy Navy SEAL.

CHUCK HADN'T TALKED about his family with anyone for a very long time, preferring not to reopen the wound. But talking about his wife and Sarah with Kate hadn't been as bad as he would've thought. Opening up had been more cathartic than painful. Perhaps the time lapse had helped to numb his response from a sharp pain to a dull ache. Either way, it felt good to get things off his chest with someone who wouldn't judge him for hiding out the past fourteen years.

Feeling a little lighter and more optimistic, he worked his way around the interior of the house, tightening the locks on the windows, replacing the ones that were missing, damaged or broken. The deadbolts took a little longer, but he installed them, and then went outside to look over the exterior of the house.

The day had warmed with bright sunshine, making him sweat.

The cottage appeared to be structurally sound with some areas of weathering that needed repair. Depending on how long they were there, he could knock out the repairs with a little manual labor, lumber, nails and paint.

As he passed the master bedroom, he could see Kate moving around inside, placing clothing from her suitcase into the dresser.

The woman was graceful, even when no one was watching. Every move flowed like a dance.

Chuck knew he should look away, but he was captivated by the sway of her hips and the way her hair fell over her shoulders and down her back.

She shook out a T-shirt and laid it on the bed. Then she unbuttoned her blouse and let it slide over her shoulders.

At that point, Chuck should have turned away. But he couldn't. He remained riveted to the window.

He was captivated by the smooth symmetry of Kate's back, the sleekness of her skin and the way her hair brushed across her shoulder blades and halfway down to her waistline.

Heat pulsed through his veins and coiled in his groin.

When she lifted the T-shirt over her head, she turned slightly, exposing the swell of her breast encased in a lacy, black bra.

A groan rose up Chuck's throat. He swallowed hard to keep from emitting it.

All he needed was to be caught behaving like a peeping Tom. He could lose his job. And worse...he would lose Kate's trust.

Though he desperately wanted to continue watching the woman, he turned away, walked to the covered patio and pulled out his cellphone.

Surprised to have any kind of reception in such a small town, he dialed Hank's number.

"Chuck. Tell me what's going on." Hank never bothered with greetings. He always got right down to business.

"Have you found anything on Kate's sister, Rachel?"

"I have Swede working on it now. He was able to hack into her phone records, but none of them led to Kate's phone number."

"Do you think she used a burner phone to contact her sister?" Chuck asked.

"That's exactly what she did. We traced the phone number she used when she called Kate the night she dropped off Lyla. From what I could tell, it was purchased in Idaho a couple days ago. No credit card records, so she probably used cash."

"Trying to hide her trail," Chuck mused. "What about her home? Have you hacked into her home phone or computer?"

"We haven't located a home phone or computer IP address." Hank continued, "We looked up the town where she supposedly lived in Idaho with her husband. It appears to be a sleepy little community in the mountains."

Chuck stiffened at the tone of Hank's voice. "You don't think it was sleepy, do you?"

"Swede found some news articles about the town. Apparently, a survivalist cult set up a compound just outside the town limits. They've stirred up the residents on a number of occasions with their religious practices and suspected abuse of their children and women."

Chuck's hand tightened around his cellphone. "Great. Have you said anything to Kate?"

"No. We're still verifying sources. Kujo and Six are between assignments. I'm sending them up there to do some snooping around."

"Good." Chuck glanced through the picture window into the living room where Lyla lay on the couch, still sleeping. "If Rachel was part of this cult, they might have returned her to the fold."

"That's what we're counting on. Kujo will go in as a hiker on vacation. With his dog Six along, it'll be more believable. They will have a good reason to be out mucking around in the mountains."

"Great. As soon as you know anything—"

"You'll be the first to get the call," Hank finished. "Other than that, everything okay at the cottage?"

"It is. The girls are settling in." Chuck smiled at Lyla sleeping on the couch. Kate entered the living room wearing the T-shirt she'd put on. And she'd pulled her long, blond hair back into a ponytail, giving her the appearance of a much younger woman.

"Let me know if you need help."

"Roger."

Hank ended the call.

Chuck slipped his cellphone into his pocket before entering the house through the back door.

Kate had entered the kitchen and set a bucket on the counter. "The place appears clean, but I'm going to do a little surface cleaning." She shrugged. "It makes me feel better to have something to do."

"Stick to the inside of the house. I'm going to jump in the shower." He nodded toward Lyla. "She should sleep for a little longer."

"We'll be fine. I'll leave the doors locked."

"Good." Chuck checked the front deadbolt once more, collected his duffel bag and strode down the hallway to the bathroom. He wouldn't take any longer than was necessary. Though the town looked sleepy and the people were friendly, he didn't know anyone well enough to trust except for the men of the Brotherhood Protectors. They were cut from the same cloth—loyal, honorable, and they had his back. Anyone else was all bets off.

CHAPTER 6

KATE CLEANED THE KITCHEN COUNTER, stove, sink and walls. Then she went to work mopping floors and dusting the furniture. Her hand in mid-swipe with a dust rag, she paused at a noise coming from the front door.

Someone knocked. Not a heavy rap but a light tap. No wonder she had barely heard it the first time.

She rose from her kneeling position by the coffee table and walked toward the front of the house, remembering Chuck's orders to leave the door locked.

Kate pulled the living room curtain to the side, hoping to see whoever it was standing at the front door.

A gray-haired little woman stood on the porch, balancing a plate stacked with sandwiches in one hand while she knocked with the other.

After a quick glance around the porch, the front walkway and the road beyond, Kate determined the woman was alone and harmless.

She hurried to answer the door.

"Oh, thank goodness," the diminutive woman sighed. "I almost dropped this plate twice, knocking." She grinned at Kate. "I'm Louise Turner. I live in the house next door. Welcome to the neighborhood." She held out the plate of sandwiches. "I would have baked a casserole, but since I just got home from a doctor's appointment, this was the quickest thing I could make in time for lunch." She shoved the plate into Kate's hands.

"Oh, thank you." Kate took the plate and smiled at the array of diagonally-cut sandwiches. "My, that's a lot of sandwiches."

"What you don't eat, you can bag and put in the refrigerator for a late-night snack. I used to make sandwiches for my husband at lunch for just that purpose. It kept me from having to get up and make them in the middle of the night when he had a hankering for a snack."

"This is a very nice treat. I was just wondering what to do for lunch." Kate noted the woman's gray hair and bright, blue eyes.

"Well, now you have it."

"Won't you join us?" Kate asked.

Mrs. Turner shook her head. "No, thank you. I know you've got a lot to do, having moved in today. I'll leave you to it. But I wanted to invite you to dinner tonight. I'm having a few people over and thought it would be nice to introduce you and your husband."

Lyla sat up on the couch and rubbed her eyes.

Mrs. Turner smiled. "Oh, and you have children as well as a dog?"

"No dog, just one child," Kate corrected. "I'm not sure what my...husband had in mind for dinner."

"Well, the offer is open. If you can make it, you're more than welcome. There won't be more than three others coming. I'd better get going. I have to water my flowers and put a roast in the crockpot." She waved at Lyla. "Hope to see you there." And Mrs. Turner was gone.

Kate was turning the lock on the front door when Chuck strode down the hallway, bare-chested and rubbing his head with a towel. And he was scowling. "Did you open the door?"

Kate held up the tray of sandwiches. "Our neighbor brought lunch and invited us to dinner."

"You shouldn't have opened the door," he said and pushed past her to check the locks and look out the window at Mrs. Turner's retreating figure.

Kate lowered her voice. "It was a little old lady, not the guy who broke into my apartment."

"You don't know if she was a setup. Did you actually *see* who broke into your apartment?"

"Well...no, but—"

"You can't be too careful. If they set her up as a decoy, they could have pushed past her as soon as you opened the door."

Kate sighed. "We don't even know if they've found us here."

"Exactly. They could have followed you here. They might know where you are and are waiting for the right time."

Lyla toddled over to where the adults were standing. "I'm hungry."

Kate stared down at the plate of sandwiches in her hand. "Do we eat them or not?"

Chuck checked out the window again.

Mrs. Turner had made it to her house and bent to pull weeds in her yard.

"She doesn't look like someone playing the part of a decoy," Kate said. But she couldn't discount the fact that Chuck was the expert bodyguard. He had experience as a witness protector.

"Let me have a bite off each one. If it doesn't kill me, you should be all right. And if I die, call Hank for a replacement bodyguard."

Kate frowned. "Are you sure?" She didn't like the idea of Chuck being the taste tester for poisoned sandwiches.

He grimaced. "You're probably right. The old lady appears to be who she says she is."

Mrs. Turner pulled a garden hose out to water the flowers in the window boxes, unaware of the people watching her.

"She invited us to dinner tonight. Should I have told her no?" Kate asked.

"If we go, we go together."

"She invited three other locals to the gathering," Kate added.

"We'll watch and see who shows up. We can decide then."

"Fair enough." Kate carried the sandwiches into the kitchen and cut a corner off all of them. She laid the corners on a plate for Chuck. "Better test these fast. Our little miss is eyeing the rest of them."

Lyla stood beside Kate, watching every move.

"Can I have little sandwiches, too?" she asked.

"After Daddy eats," Kate said.

"Are you going to eat now, Daddy?" Lyla asked. She licked her lips, staring at the plate of sandwich corners.

"Yes, ma'am." He grinned down at her. "Why don't you wash up while I see if these are as good as they look?"

"Okay," she said and ran off to the bathroom to wash her hands.

"I'll go help her. I think the sink is a little high for her to reach."

"I'll build her a step to stand on," he said and took a bite of one of the corners Kate had cut from the sandwiches.

Kate froze, her gaze on his face, watching, praying he didn't fall over dead after having been poisoned by an old woman.

"Hmmm," he tilted his head and tugged at his collar. Then he coughed and opened his eyes wide.

Kate's heart raced. "What? Are you all right? Was it poisoned?"

Chuck swallowed and laughed. "I'm sorry, I shouldn't tease you. But you looked so concerned, I couldn't help it."

"You're awful!" Kate grabbed his arm and shook it. "Don't do that. I think I lost a year off my life."

His smile faded. "I'm sorry. That was mean of me.

But the good news is, the sandwiches aren't killing me. Mrs. Turner is probably just who she said she was."

Kate drew in a shaky breath. "Still, I'm not sure I want to feed Lyla any of the sandwiches for another hour or so."

"Just to make sure it's not a slow-acting poison?" He chuckled. "Glad to know you care."

With a snort, Kate turned toward the bathroom. "It would serve you right if you dropped dead, choking on a sandwich."

His laughter followed her all the way to the bathroom, the sound warming her insides more than she cared to admit.

The man was entirely too attractive and had a wicked sense of humor. In her mind, that was a killer combination, and she wasn't sure she could resist it for long.

CHUCK MADE fresh sandwiches for Lyla and Kate, while they were busy in the bathroom. By the time they emerged, he'd set the table with plates, glasses of ice and napkins.

"Have a seat, ladies," he said. He held the chair for Lyla and helped her into it. "Would you like water or juice?"

"Juice," Lyla said.

"Water for me." Kate took her seat, her gaze on the plate of sandwiches. "Are those different than the ones Mrs. Turner brought?"

"Yes, ma'am. I didn't want you to worry, so I made

them specially for my girls." He winked at Lyla and placed Mrs. Turner's sandwiches in front of his plate. "I'll take care of these."

Kate helped herself and Lyla to the ones Chuck had prepared while he poured juice into Lyla's cup and filled Kate's with tap water.

Then they sat at the table like a family.

Chuck took one of Mrs. Turner's sandwiches and let the image of Kate and Lyla sink in.

God, he missed having a family. Why hadn't he moved on? He felt as if he'd been in a holding pattern for so long, he didn't know how to land.

For the next twenty minutes, he pretended to be a father to Lyla and a husband to Kate.

And it felt good.

At the end of the meal, he helped Kate clean the table and wash the dishes by hand. The cozy cottage was mid-last-century-dated. No dishwasher existed in the small kitchen.

Chuck insisted on washing. Kate and Lyla dried the dishes and put them in the cabinet.

Thankfully, Sadie had included four place settings of dishes and flatware. They wouldn't have to resort to paper plates and plastic forks to eat, unless they wanted to.

That afternoon, they worked on organizing their few belongings and the toys Sadie had sent.

Kate opted for a long soak in the clawfoot tub while Chuck kept an eye on Lyla. All the while Kate was in the bathroom, Chuck couldn't help but imagine her naked body lying in a scented bath.

Chuck had to get a grip on his attraction to his client or risk jeopardizing the mission. He needed to focus on keeping Kate and Lyla safe.

The sun was setting when Kate emerged from the bedroom wearing a simple, white dress that hugged her torso and flared out around her legs. The fabric lay softly against her and swayed when she moved.

Chuck had helped Lyla into one of the pretty dresses Sadie had given her and pulled her blond hair up into a single ponytail, twisting the strands into a smooth braid.

Kate smiled and shook her head. "You are good at being a daddy."

"She's a good kid and stayed really still while I brushed her hair."

"He doesn't hurt me when I have tangles," Lyla said. She smiled up at Kate. "You're pretty, Mama."

Kate's cheeks blushed a rosy pink as she curtsied in front of her niece. "Thank you. And so are you."

"Isn't Daddy pretty?" Lyla slipped her hand into Chuck's.

"Yes, Lyla. Daddy's pretty, too."

Chuck frowned, though his lips twitched on the corners. "Handsome. Boys aren't pretty."

Lyla tipped her head to one side and looked up at Chuck. "Why?"

Kate didn't help. She raised her brows and crossed her arms over her chest. "Seriously. Why?"

Chuck tugged at the button-up shirt he'd changed into for the dinner at Mrs. Turner's. "Never mind. We'll be late for dinner if we don't leave now."

"How do you know?" Kate asked, but she dropped her arms to her sides and draped a sweater over her arm. "I don't recall Mrs. Turner setting a time."

"I saw an older couple and a woman enter her house a few minutes ago. I assume those are the guests she spoke of."

"Probably." Kate said. "I'm ready."

Together, they walked next door to Mrs. Turner's house.

She met them at the door, smiling broadly. "I'm so glad you decided to come. Please, come in and meet my friends."

When Kate stepped inside and Chuck followed, Mrs. Turner stared at him and frowned. "Oh."

Chuck's brows furrowed. "Is something wrong?"

She shook her head, the frown still firmly set. "I don't think so. It's just you aren't who I expected."

Kate tilted her head. "What do you mean?"

"You're not the man I saw walking the dog earlier. I thought that man was your husband."

"I'm sorry," Kate said. "What man?"

"There was a man walking a dog on our road earlier today. He was shorter, not as big." Mrs. Turner held her hands out demonstrating how broad the other man's shoulders were. "And he was bald." She pointed to Chuck's head. "You have a full head of hair. I know I wasn't seeing things."

"Whoever it was, wasn't my husband," Kate said. "Is it unusual for someone to walk his dog on this road?"

Mrs. Turner shrugged. "Not unusual, just unusual to

have new people move in next door and a stranger walk down the road on the same day."

One of the older women smiled. "We're a small town. Not much changes."

Her husband cupped her elbow and laughed. "But when it does...we notice." He held out his hand. "Hugh Landry."

Kate gripped his hand. "Kate—"

"Johnson," Chuck cut in. "Kate, Lyla and Chuck Johnson."

Mr. Landry shook Chuck's hand next. "This is my wife Greta and our friend, Wanda Wilcox."

The introductions over, Mrs. Turner led the way into the dining room. The aroma of roast beef and onions filled the air and made Chuck's mouth water.

"Please have a seat," Mrs. Turner said.

Chuck helped Lyla into one of the chairs, and then held another for Kate. He helped Mrs. Turner with her chair, and then sat on the other side of Lyla, figuring they could better meet her needs if they worked as a team.

Kate settled Lyla's napkin in her lap and one in her own.

"You're just in time," Mrs. Turner said. "We were about to sit down for dinner."

"Would you carve?" Mrs. Turner passed the carving knife to Chuck, and soon, they were passing plates and platters of food around until everyone had been served.

The conversation was lively, the older guests filling them in on the gossip about other members of the community.

Chuck didn't recognize any of the names, but he listened in case he heard something that might concern him, Kate or Lyla.

"Your dog-walking man might be one of the men here working the pipeline construction," Wanda said. "Rita's Bed & Breakfast has been booked solid for the past couple of weeks. I expect they'll be moving on, once they complete the section they're working north of town."

"The Blue Moose Tavern has been pretty busy lately with them and some people getting a jump on the tourist season. We already have hikers up in the Crazy Mountains. The forestry service had to rescue some just yesterday."

"Wow," Kate's fork paused halfway to her mouth. "Was someone lost?"

"No, but a hiker got crossways with a mama bear. The bear won, and the hiker had to be air-lifted out."

"Wow. I hadn't thought about bears." Kate's gaze met Chuck's over Lyla's head.

"Don't worry, we haven't had a bear in Eagle Rock in over ten years."

"Only ten years?" Kate gulped.

"We emphasize bear awareness," Mrs. Turner said. "Don't leave your trash out in bags. Use bear-proof trash cans. Don't leave your pets out at night. Not so much because of the bears but because of the wolves and coyotes."

"I lost my malti-poo, Sweetpea, because she wandered out of the yard one evening. I think a coyote got her." Wanda sniffed. "I miss that little dog."

Greta patted her friend's hand. "We all miss Sweetpea. She was a good, little dog."

"Goes the same for children," Hugh said. "Don't leave them unattended outside."

Chuck had no intention of leaving Lyla unattended. Not only because of the wild animals, but because of the threat from whoever was after Kate's sister.

"I suppose the man with the dog could be one of the pipeline workers. I won't worry about him." Mrs. Turner smiled at Kate and Chuck. "We look out for each other here. Being on the edge of town, no one would think much of us. JoJo Earles was the previous owner of the cottage you're living in. She was a lovely woman and a good friend. We miss her dearly, don't we?" Mrs. Turner's gaze swept over her older friends, who nodded their agreement.

"Did she pass away?" Kate asked.

Mrs. Turner laughed. "Oh, dear. No, she didn't. Her children moved her to Florida. They were afraid she'd slip on the ice in the wintertime and no one would find her until she'd frozen to death."

Kate's eyes rounded. "That would be awful."

Mrs. Turner nodded. "That's why we look out for each other."

"Now that JoJo's gone, will you be moving south to live with your daughter in Alabama?" Wanda asked.

"No way," Mrs. Turner shook her head. "I like my independence. I don't plan on losing that until I can't take care of myself."

"Well, I must say I feel a lot better now that you have

good neighbors living next door," Hugh said. "Someone looking out for you."

Kate cast a glance toward Chuck, her jaw tight, her eyes sad.

"We'll do what we can," Chuck said. "After all, what are neighbors for?" He nearly choked on the words he figured they would expect out of him. What he didn't add was the disclaimer of *while we're here.*

The dinner was tasty, the company warm and inviting. But by the time it was over, Chuck was ready to leave and so was Lyla.

"I'm sleepy." She yawned and stretched. "Can we go home now?"

Kate gave Mrs. Turner an apologetic smile. "I'm sorry. She's had a big day with us moving in."

"Oh, please. Don't you worry about it. I had three children of my own. You're on their schedule while they're little."

Wanda chuckled. "And well into their twenties."

"So true," Hugh agreed.

Greta sighed. "I miss my boys."

"I'll be glad when they return to the states," Hugh said. "We'll meet them in Virginia when they come home."

"Where are they?" Chuck asked.

"They're in the Navy. They're deployed now to the Horn of Africa."

Chuck perked up. "I'd love to hear more, but we need to get Lyla to bed. Perhaps next time?"

"Oh, you won't get Hugh to quit talking about David

and Michael," Greta said. "He's so proud of their accomplishments. They're Navy SEALs."

Chuck's chest swelled, but he didn't tell them that he had once been a Navy SEAL on active duty. They didn't need to know that. No one needed to know. As far as he was concerned, he was Kate's husband and Lyla's father. The less Lyla's attackers knew, the better. And the only way to keep that information from them was to keep as much to himself as possible.

He lifted Lyla into his arms and carried her toward the door.

Kate caught up and slipped her arm through his empty one. They walked away from Mrs. Turner's little white, clapboard house and into their yellow cottage, a family for all to see.

Once inside the house, Kate took Lyla and carried her into the bedroom with the twin bed and helped her change into her pajamas.

Chuck went around the house one more time, checking all the windows and doors. He regretted that there were so many windows. If someone wanted in badly enough, all he had to do was break one window.

Chuck could hear Kate's voice as she read a story from one of the books Sadie had packed in a box.

He stood outside Lyla's room, listening to the clear, sweet sound of her voice and wishing she was talking to him in the shadows as they lay in bed. He would hold her in his arms, close his eyes and just bask in the smooth silkiness of her tone.

Kate tiptoed backward out of Lyla's room, pulling the door halfway closed. When she turned toward

Chuck, she started, her hand flying to her mouth. "Oh. I didn't see you there."

"I'm sorry I scared you."

Her hand dropped to her chest. "No. I'm okay." She looked back through the door. "Poor thing was so tired, she didn't make it through the entire book."

"She's had a tough twenty-four hours. A lot of changes."

Kate nodded, her gaze rising to Chuck's. "She's holding it together much better than I am." Her eyes filled with tears. "I wish I knew my sister was safe."

Without letting himself think, Chuck pulled her into his arms and held her.

Kate laid her cheek against his chest and let the tears fall. "I should be braver," she said and sniffed. "Lyla needs me to be strong."

"You don't have to be strong all the time," he said, stroking his hand over her soft hair. "That's why you have me."

"Thank you for being here," she said, her fingers curling into his shirt. "I don't think I could do this without your help."

"It's what I do. It's my job," he said, as much to reassure her as to remind himself he could not fall for this woman. She was a client. Nothing more.

Then why was his heart beating so fast? And why was he still holding her in his arms?

CHAPTER 7

KATE WOULD HAVE STAYED in Chuck's arms for as long as he would let her, but Lyla made a noise that brought her back to reality.

"I'd better check on her," Kate said and slipped from Chuck's arms. Back in Lyla's room, Kate called herself all kinds of a fool for taking advantage of Chuck. The man was only holding her to make her feel safer. He wasn't making any other kind of move on her, nor did she expect him to.

He was a man of honor and wouldn't take advantage of the situation to slake his own desires.

Heat coiled low in her belly. Oh, but she wished he would take advantage of her. Her desire was strong and getting stronger.

Lyla twisted in the sheets, trying to kick them off.

When Kate pulled the blankets back up over her, the little girl squirmed and moaned.

Was she having a nightmare?

In the faint glow spilling in through the half-opened door, Lyla's cheeks glowed a ruddy red.

Kate touched her forehead and felt the heat. Lyla was burning up.

"Chuck," she called out.

He was there in a heartbeat, looking over her shoulder at the small child lying against the white sheets, her face coated in a sheen of sweat.

"She's feverish," Kate said. "What do we do?"

He touched his palm to her forehead, his eyebrows drawing together. "A cool compress will help." Without another word, he hurried to the bathroom across the hall and returned a minute later with a cool, damp washcloth.

Gently, he laid the cloth across Lyla's forehead.

"Was there a thermometer in any of those boxes Sadie sent?" Chuck asked.

"I don't know," Kate said, her gaze on Lyla. "Wait. She sent a first aid kit. Maybe there's one in it." Kate rose from beside the bed and ran into the kitchen. Where had she put that little, red box? She'd been so caught up in watching Chuck fix the doors and windows earlier that day, she hadn't paid much attention to where she was putting things.

After searching three kitchen drawers, she finally found the first aid kit in a deep drawer next to the sink. Inside the kit was a thermometer. She grabbed it and ran back into Lyla's room.

"Here it is." She held it out to Chuck, who took it and rolled Lyla onto her back.

"How are you going to get her to hold it under her tongue?" Kate asked.

Chuck shook his head. "I'm not."

He pulled Lyla's pajama top up and placed the thermometer under her arm. He waited a solid minute before he removed the thermometer and pulled Lyla's shirt back in place before staring down at the number in the display.

"One hundred degrees," Chuck said. "It's not good, but it could be worse."

"What should we do?" Kate asked. "I don't recall seeing a hospital in town."

"There isn't one," Chuck confirmed.

Kate paced the length of the room, her head down, her lips pressed tight. She stopped in front of Chuck. "Do we need to take her to the ER in Bozeman?"

"I think we need to see where it goes. If she gets worse, then yes, we take her to another town where they have an emergency room." Chuck lifted the damp cloth, fanned it to cool it off, and then laid it back on Lyla's forehead. "In the meantime, I'll stay up with her. You should get some sleep. We don't know what tomorrow will bring. You need to be physically prepared for anything."

When Kate didn't move, Chuck gripped her arms. "Go to bed."

"But I can't leave Lyla while she's sick." Kate shook loose of Chuck's grip and slipped around him to enter Lyla's room.

Her niece lay like a miniature ghost, her face red and her entire body flushed with heat.

"Will she be okay?" Kate's words caught in her throat on a sob. The one job she had to do was to keep Lyla safe. How could she keep her safe if she was so sick?

"We should take her to the hospital in Bozeman," Kate insisted.

"The doctors don't start worrying until a child's temperature spikes to over one hundred and three. Lyla's not there yet."

"But should we wait that long?" Kate smoothed her hand over Lyla's angel-soft hair. "I don't want anything bad to happen to my niece. Rachel trusted me to do the right thing." Kate snorted. "She should have known I don't have a clue about what the right thing is regarding small children."

"Like I said, the doctors aren't much concerned until the fever spikes to over one hundred and three."

"Then I'm staying with her all night."

"That won't be necessary. I'll stay with her," Chuck said. "I consider it my duty and responsibility."

"As her aunt, it's my duty and responsibility," Kate insisted, lifting her chin. "I should be with her."

"Rather than argue over a sick little girl, how about we take turns?" He raised his brow. "I'll take the first shift until one in the morning."

"And you'll wake me when it's my turn?" She stared at him through narrowed eyes. "You won't try to be all tough-guy on me, will you?"

"What do you mean?"

She lifted her chin. "You won't just say you'll wake me but actually leave me to sleep all night?"

Chuck laughed and raised his hand. "Scout's honor,"

he said.

Kate's frown deepened. "Something tells me you were never a scout."

"You have my word," Chuck said. "I'll wake you."

"Okay, then." She leaned over Lyla and kissed her forehead. "I hope you feel better soon, sweetie. I love you." Then she straightened and pointed a finger at Chuck's chest. "Wake me for anything."

Chuck smiled. "Yes, ma'am."

If Lyla wasn't feverish and Kate wasn't worried, she might have melted into the floor. Chuck had charm all wrapped up in that smile.

Kate glanced once more at Lyla, reluctant to leave the child's room. Could a three-year-old die from a fever? Her heart squeezed hard in her chest. Rachel would be devastated. Hell, Kate would be devastated. Lyla was growing on her, as well as the idea of having a child in her life. Her career seemed so secondary to the responsibility of a little girl's life.

Kate hurried to the bedroom, changed into her nightgown and lay down on the bed. For the next thirty minutes, she stared at the ceiling, imagining every scenario that could happen. The more she lay there, the more worried she became. Sounds made her jump, thinking it might be Lyla calling for her or Chuck asking for help.

When she couldn't take another minute, she grabbed the comforter from the bed and padded barefooted down the hall and peeked in on Lyla.

Chuck had moved a rocking chair into the room and set it beside Lyla's bed. He sat still and held Lyla's hand with one of his and brushed the hair from her fevered brow with the other.

Not wanting to disturb them, Kate quietly laid the comforter on the floor and curled up inside it. If she was needed, she'd be there. If anything changed, she'd know immediately.

Exhausted from her mad escape from LA and her subsequent journey to Montana, Kate fell into a deep sleep.

In the middle of the night, her sleep became troubled with dreams about men in black ski masks, breaking into the little cottage to steal Lyla away.

She tried to tell them Lyla was sick. If they took her she could die. But they didn't care. They grabbed Lyla from her bed and ran.

Kate cried out, horrified and heartbroken, but unable to go after them. Her feet felt mired in quicksand. When she looked down, she couldn't see her shoes. They had sunk into the floor of her executive office, and she was being sucked into the carpet, inch by inch. "Lyla!" she called out.

Lyla couldn't help her. She was only a small child.

"Chuck!" she called out, her cries turning to sobs.

Warm arms wrapped around her and held her against a solid wall of muscles.

"Shh, darlin'," a deep, resonant voice whispered in her ear. "Everything is going to be all right."

"But Lyla..." she said without opening her eyes.

"Is asleep in her bed. The fever broke, and she's sleeping soundly."

Kate pressed her face into her rescuer's chest and let the tears flow until there were none left to fall.

Warm lips pressed against her forehead. "You're going to be okay," he promised.

"How do you know?" she whispered, unwilling to wake up from the dream. The arms around her felt so real and comforting. She wanted to stay there forever.

"I know, because I'll make it happen. Lyla's going to be fine. Just sleep."

"Mmm." She rested her hand on his chest and curled her fingers into his shirt.

Strong arms lifted her from the floor, comforter and all.

At that point, Kate realized she was no longer sleeping and Chuck was her rescuer. Still, she refused to open her eyes, preferring to bask in the reality of being in his arms.

When he laid Kate on her bed and started to straighten, she finally opened her eyes and stared up into his. "Are you sure Lyla's okay?"

He nodded and swept the hair out of her face, tucking it behind her ear. "Her temperature is back to normal. She's sleeping peacefully."

Then he did something she never expected.

He bent and brushed his lips across hers.

Kate froze, her eyes widening.

"Sorry," he said. "I just can't…" And he kissed her again.

Kate raised her hand to his chest. Not to push him away, but to clutch his shirt and bring him back to her mouth. She tipped her head and kissed him back.

He wrapped his hand around the back of her head and held her to him as his lips pressed against hers and his tongue traced the seam of her mouth.

She opened on an exhilarated gasp, allowing him to sweep in and own her tongue.

He caressed, teased and stroked her, tasting of mint and the tea he'd had at dinner.

Kate couldn't get enough of him. She clung to Chuck, holding him close, reluctant to let go.

And he seemed in no hurry to release her.

He sat on the edge of the bed and gathered her closer, pulling her across his lap, deepening the kiss. His hands slipped down her back and up her sides, his thumbs brushing below her breasts.

A moan rose up her throat and escaped. God, she wanted more from this man than just a kiss.

When he at last raised his head, she stared up at him in wonder. What had just happened seemed almost a part of a dream. Not the nightmare he'd rescued her from, but a sweet, lusty dream she wanted to go back to.

"We shouldn't have done that," he said.

"No, we shouldn't have." But she was glad they had. And she wanted to kiss him all over again. Her body physically ached for him.

Chuck straightened. "I'll sleep on the couch."

"You don't have to, you know." Kate wished he would take her up on her hint and stay with her in the bed.

He stood tall and straight, his jaw tight, his hands curled into fists as if he struggled with something difficult. "You tempt me," he said, his voice deep and sexy.

"But I can't." He shook his head and performed an about-face. "I'll check on Lyla on my way to the couch."

"Chuck?"

He turned back.

"I know we shouldn't have…but I'm glad we did."

CHUCK STARED at Kate for a moment longer, drinking in her beauty and the swell of her very-kissed lips. Then he turned and walked away.

A thousand thoughts rippled through his mind at once. Images of his wife the last time he saw her flashed through his memory. She'd stood with Sarah, seeing him off as he boarded the bus that would take his team to catch the plane to Afghanistan.

She'd smiled, though her eyes shone with unshed tears.

Sarah had waved goodbye, and then held up her arms for Anne to carry her.

As the bus pulled away, Chuck watched them as long as he could, knowing it would be months before he saw them again. He hadn't dreamed it would be the last time he saw his wife and child.

Now, after kissing Kate, he could see the potential for pain and heartache happening again. Kate and Lyla reminded him so much of Anne and Sarah, in appearances anyway.

Anne had been a stay-at-home wife and mother to their child. She'd been content to manage the household and greet him with open arms and a hearty meal when he came home.

Anne had no ambition for working outside the home. Chuck had worried she would be lonely with him gone most of the time. And she had been. Her world revolved around him. Each time he left on a mission, she would be sad and depressed. He'd tried to get her to join the military wives club, but she preferred staying home. Knowing she was unhappy made it hard for Chuck to focus on his work.

Kate, on the other hand, was a woman who had a successful career, no children, no marriages. She took charge and could stand on her own.

Chuck believed Kate could protect herself and Lyla without him. But she was smart enough to know it helped having someone else around to cover her back.

She was beautiful, confident and intelligent. And that kiss...

He was in deep trouble. As soon as he'd touched her lips, he'd known there was no going back. He had to kiss her again.

Now, he was running scared. Scared he was falling for a woman after all the years he'd sworn off love, marriage and family. He didn't believe in happily-ever-after. Not after losing Anne and Sarah.

He stopped on the way down the hall to duck into Lyla's room.

She lay with her arm wrapped around Sid Sloth, her stuffed animal.

Chuck held his breath and felt her forehead. Cool and dry.

He let go of the breath on a sigh. Thank goodness, she was okay. He left her door open and made another pass through the house, testing the door locks and the window latches. He stood by the front window, staring out at the night.

On the edge of town, the little cottage wasn't inundated with street lights. Stars shone down, providing enough light to illuminate the road and houses. But there were deep shadows he couldn't see into.

Had Lyla's pursuers traced them to Montana? Would they catch up to them soon?

Chuck's hands clenched into fists.

He wouldn't let anything happen to Lyla and Kate. Not on his watch.

A soft hand touched his shoulder.

Kate stood behind him.

He didn't have to turn to see her. He could tell it was her by the scent of spring flowers.

"Are you worried they've found us?" she whispered.

"I have to think of all the possibilities," he answered.

"Thank you for being here for us," she said. "I couldn't have done this on my own."

He shook his head. "You would have found a way."

She emitted a gentle snort. "I would have done my best, but there's so much I don't know about protecting a child and taking care of her."

"You're doing fine by letting her know you love her. That's all she needs."

Her lips curled upward. "And Sid Sloth."

Kate's smile melted Chuck's heart. He turned and gripped her arms. "I don't know what happened a moment ago, but we can't let it happen again."

She stared up at him, her eyes wide. "No," she breathed, her lips rosy from their kiss. "We can't."

His control was slipping, and he struggled to regain it. "I'm serious." He shook her gently.

She raised her hands to his waist, nodding. "I know."

"Then why can't I resist?" he said. "Oh, hell." All reason flew out the window, and he lowered his mouth to hers, crushing her lips with a kiss both desperate and beautiful.

He gathered her close in his arms, pulling her body flush against his.

She wrapped her arms around his middle and held on, giving back as much as he gave.

When he traced her lips with the tip of his tongue, she opened to him, letting him in.

Chuck thrust in, claiming her mouth, tasting her in a long, sensuous caress. Their tongues tangled and twisted around each other while their hands explored.

Kate slipped her fingers beneath his shirt and splayed them across his back. They were warm and strong, kneading into his flesh.

He dragged the hem of her nightgown over her hips and slid his hands across her lower back, loving the silkiness of her skin.

His groin tightened, and his shaft swelled, pressing against her taut belly.

Kate's hands shifted lower and into the waistband of his jeans.

Chuck moaned. "Don't go there if you don't mean it," he said against her lips.

"I mean it," she whispered into his mouth, and her

tongue thrust between his teeth and tangled again with his.

Bending, he scooped her up by the backs of her thighs and wrapped her legs around his waist. Then he backed her against a wall and deepened the kiss, like a man drinking from a bottomless well. He wanted to be closer…couldn't get enough of Kate.

She wrapped her arms around his neck and wove her hands into his hair.

"I want you," he said.

"Inside me," she agreed. "Now."

"Protection." That he could think about it was a miracle. But he refused to risk bringing another child into the world because he was careless.

She leaned back, a frown puckering her brow. "You have some?"

"Back pocket." He kissed the column of her throat and nibbled on her earlobe. "Wallet."

Kate slipped her hand into his back pocket and extracted his wallet. While he feasted on her neck, she pulled out a foil packet and slipped his wallet back into his pocket.

She tore open the packet and pressed her hands against his chest.

He held her far enough away from him that she could reach the button and zipper on his jeans. In seconds, she had flipped open the rivet and slid the tab down.

Unfettered by denim, his cock sprang free.

She laughed. "Commando?"

Chuck growled. "Damn right."

Her smile faded as she hurriedly rolled the condom over him. Then she captured his cheeks between her palms and looked him square in the eye. "Foreplay is overrated."

"Sweet Jesus, yes!" he pushed aside her panties and nudged her with the tip of his staff.

Kate was slick with her own juices, ripe and ready for him.

He eased into her and paused, the act taking all his diminishing control. "Say no, and it stops here." He could barely say the words. His chest was so tight, and his body was on fire with need.

"Don't stop now," she cried. "I've never been so... so...on fire."

He thrust into her, pushing deep until he could go no farther. Drawing in a deep breath, he waited, letting her adjust to his girth.

Kate wasn't waiting for long. She pressed down on his shoulders, lifting up his shaft, only to ease down again. "Yes, please," she said as she exhaled and dragged in another ragged breath.

After another slow glide in and out, he couldn't hold back any longer. He leaned her against the wall, grabbed her hips and thrust into her, hard and fast.

"Better," she said and held on for the ride.

Chuck powered into her like a piston on a racecar engine, pounding her as hard and as fast as he could and still balance her. A bed would have been easier, but he couldn't take the time to move her there. Not when he was so...very...close.

One more thrust, and he shot over the precipice. He

drove deep, clutching her bottom, digging his fingers into her flesh as he held on, milking the orgasm to the very last shudder.

Kate kissed his forehead, his temple and his eyelids. "Wow," she said. "That was amazing."

His desire slaked for the moment, regret set in. Part of the beauty of making love to a woman was watching her lose herself in the process. "I should have gotten you there first."

She swept a hand through his hair. "I didn't need you to. It felt good."

"We aren't done yet," he said and carried her to the floral couch, still deep inside her. Instead of laying her on the cushion, he perched her bottom on the back of the couch and pulled free. After disposing of the condom, he spread her legs and stepped between. "Now, it's your turn."

CHAPTER 8

Kate balanced on the back of the couch, her channel slick with her juices, and her core coiled and ready for whatever Chuck had in mind. "Aren't you afraid we'll wake Lyla?" she asked, her gaze going to the hallway and the open door.

"If we didn't wake her before, she'll sleep through this." He stepped back. "But I'll check on her. Don't move."

He zipped his jeans and hurried to the bedroom.

Kate took the moment to shed her panties and stuff them into the cushions of the couch. Chuck had moved them aside to make love to her, but she didn't want anything in the way of what he might have in mind next.

She waited, her breath catching in her throat, her heart pounding hard against her ribs.

The few short moments he stepped away gave her

entirely too much time to think about what she was doing.

What was she thinking? This man was hired to protect her, not to make love to her. If she was smart, she'd pull on her panties and hightail it back to her bed. Alone.

But she wasn't thinking with her mind. Her body burned for more and wouldn't let her leave the couch to save her soul.

When Chuck returned, he stalked toward her like a tiger on the prowl for its prey. His eyes narrowed as he studied her face. "Having second thoughts?"

She nodded, her throat tightening to the point she couldn't push air past her vocal cords.

He parted her legs again and stepped between her knees. Then he cupped the back of her head and tipped her head up, forcing her to meet his gaze. "Want me to change your mind?"

His deep tone resonated through the room, making her nerves spontaneously combust and shoot electrical pulses throughout her system.

She wanted him to do wicked things to her.

"Please," she said.

"Please what?" He lifted the hem of her nightgown but didn't pull it up over her head.

Kate raised her arms. "Please, change my mind."

Chuck ripped the gown over her head and flung it across the room. For a long moment, his gaze swept her body, taking in every curve and swell.

Kate's nipples puckered, and her core heated. She held her breath in anticipation.

He reached out and lifted the necklace she'd worn beneath her nightgown. "Do you always wear this?" His knuckles grazed the swells of her breasts.

Dragging a deep breath to steady her pounding heart, she nodded. "Hank told me to wear it always. I think it has a tracking device in it."

"Smart man." He lifted the pendant and touched his lips to it. "You're beautiful."

She started to raise her arms to cover her bare breasts.

"Don't." Chuck captured her wrists and held them for a moment.

Kate raised her eyebrows, a shiver rippling across her skin. "I seem to be the only naked one here."

He winked. "But you do it so well." Then he pulled off his shirt and flung it to join her nightgown. "I'd go further, but it might be harder to explain my being naked to a three-year-old."

"True."

"And I don't need to be naked to do this." He bent to press his lips to the base of her throat. "Or this," he whispered against her beating pulse. His mouth slipped over her collarbone and down to capture a nipple between his teeth.

For the next few moments, he nibbled, nipped and flicked that nipple.

Kate moaned softly and clutched the back of his head, her fingers digging into his scalp.

"Like that?" he asked.

"Yesss..." She leaned her head back and let him have his way with that nipple and then the other.

By the time he abandoned them, she was squirming on the back of the couch, ready for him to take it downward.

And he did.

Chuck dropped to his knees and dragged his lips over her ribs, one at a time. He dipped his tongue into her belly button and continued downward to the fluff of hair at the juncture of her thighs.

Kate widened her legs automatically, her breathing ragged, her pulse racing.

Parting her folds with his fingers, Chuck leaned in and blew a warm stream of air over that heated strip of flesh.

Kate gasped and applied pressure to the back of his head, urging him to do more.

With his tongue, he flicked her clit, sending a jolt of electricity racing across her body.

"Oh my," she whispered.

He tapped that spot with the tip of his tongue, teasing her to the point she wanted to scream.

"Please," she begged.

Chuckling, he ran his tongue across her sweet spot again and again until she dropped her hands to her knees, pulled back her legs and gave in to the orgasm that rocked her to her very soul.

Chuck curled one hand behind her to keep her from toppling over the back of the couch while the other spread her folds for the magic of his mouth.

For what felt like a lifetime and yet was so short it could only have been a length of a breath, Kate flew to the heavens and back, her body spasming, her hips rocking to the rhythm of Chuck's tongue.

When she floated back to earth, she couldn't have remembered her name, where she was from or the color of summer grass.

Chuck rose from his knees, stood her on her feet, then left her to gather their clothes from where they'd landed on the floor.

With care and kisses, he dressed her in her nightgown, guiding the fabric over her head, across her shoulders and down her torso, his hands touching her skin all the way.

Kate sighed and leaned into him, her legs like jelly, her body completely relaxed against his. "Wow."

A warm chuckle reverberated between them. "I've never known a woman to come that completely undone."

"I've never come so close to dying." She lay her head against his chest, listening to the rapid beat of his heart. "I believe you've ruined me."

"How so?"

"I don't think anything can top that."

"No?" He tipped back her head and brushed a strand of her hair back behind her ear.

"Not even ice cream," she said, her brain fuzzy, her body still humming from her incredible experience.

Chuck laughed out loud, and then slapped his hand over his mouth. "I'll take that as a compliment. Better than ice cream?"

"Mmm-hmmm." She lifted up on her toes and pressed her lips to his. They tasted of her. It made her tingle down there again. And if she didn't step away soon, she'd beg him to do it all again.

A soft sound came from the bedroom down the hallway, pulling her out of the spell he'd cast on her.

Kate sighed. "I'll check on Lyla."

"I'll make another round of the house," Chuck said. "And then we need to get some sleep. We don't know what tomorrow will bring."

Kate smiled. "You mean today." She nodded toward a clock on the wall.

"Right." He winced. "And children have a habit of getting up at the crack of dawn."

Though she knew she needed to check on Lyla, Kate found it difficult to let go of Chuck. She had the feeling that once she did, everything would change. Things would go back to the way they were before. Him being the bodyguard, her being the client. Purely professional.

Oh, but they'd crossed that bridge and there was no going back. Not for Kate.

CHUCK CHECKED the windows and doors once again, even though he'd done it only minutes before. It gave him an excuse to step away from Kate. If he stood too close to her, he'd be too tempted to keep her in his arms and make love to her all over again.

They had been very lucky that Lyla hadn't walked in on them while they were in the heat of passion. Witnessing people who aren't her parents getting it on would be hard to comprehend at her age. And Chuck was certain Kate's sister wouldn't appreciate them exposing themselves to the little girl.

He ran a hand down his face. This lack of control wasn't like him. Being focused was what he did, how he'd stayed alive on all the missions he'd conducted with the Navy SEALs and on special assignment with the DEA. He'd done whatever had to be done to accomplish his mission. Emotions and relationships couldn't get in the way. People died when one lost focus.

Kate emerged from Lyla's room and stood in the hallway. Her nightgown hung down to mid-thigh.

Chuck knew she wasn't wearing underwear and vaguely wondered where she'd ditched them. But it didn't matter. She wasn't wearing any, and it made him hard all over again.

"Go to bed," he said, his tone a lot sterner than he intended.

Kate nodded, as if she understood his struggle. She turned and walked barefooted to the master bedroom, her shoulders back, her head high.

God, she was beautiful.

With every ounce of self-control he could muster, Chuck resisted following Kate and making love to her for the rest of what was left of the night.

They didn't need Lyla waking up to find them naked in bed together. They could do without that kind of trauma. The kid had enough stacked against her as it was.

He settled in the lounge chair and kicked up the footrest. Day One on the new job had seen him set up house with a beautiful woman and child, go to dinner with the old people of the town and make love to his client. It wasn't a SEAL mission or busting a drug dealer, but it might be the most important mission of his life. He'd better get his shit together before someone got hurt.

He suspected it might be him. Already, his heart was on the line. *After only one day.*

Closing his eyes, he willed himself to catch some shuteye. He'd learned the skill of falling asleep quickly as a young Navy SEAL. He drew on that skill now to keep his body refreshed and ready to go should the need arise.

HE MUST HAVE SLEPT, because when he opened his eyes again, sun shone around the curtains hanging in the windows and tiny footsteps sounded in the hallway.

Lyla stood in the middle of the hallway, her stuffed sloth clutched to her chest, her eyes wide, scared.

"Hey, Lyla," Chuck called out softly. "It's okay. You can come sit with me until…Mama wakes up."

She stared at him for a long time.

Chuck sat up, folding the leg rest under him.

Lyla remained standing in the hallway, her bottom lip quivering.

His heart squeezed hard in his chest. "Oh, baby. It's okay," he tried to reassure her. "Did you have a bad dream?"

She nodded.

Chuck held out his arms. "Come here. Nothing can hurt you while you're with me."

Lyla took in a shaky breath, and then ran toward him.

He rose from his chair in time to catch her as she flung herself into his arms.

"Oh, sweetheart, you're going to be just fine." Chuck held her close, rocking back and forth from one foot to the other. "You're in a new house, in a new place, and everything takes a little getting used to."

She wrapped her arms around his neck and buried her face against him, Sid Sloth crushed between them. Her body was stiff in his arms, as if she was tight with fear.

After a while, Lyla relaxed and loosened her grip around his neck.

Chuck crossed to the window to let in the sunshine. Everything seemed to get better when the sun was shining. The sun would scare away the shadows where bad things hid.

Lyla sat up and stared out the window, her sloth clutched under her chin.

"Feeling better?" Chuck asked.

She nodded.

"Hungry?"

Again, she nodded.

Still carrying Lyla, he entered the kitchen, then found a bowl and the cereal they'd purchased at the grocery store. He carried Lyla to the table. When he tried to place her in one of the seats, she refused to let go of him.

"Okay then." He chuckled. "We'll just make a few more trips. No worries." Chuck ferried milk, a cup, a bowl and a spoon to the table. Once he had everything set out, he took his seat and settled Lyla in his lap. "Want to move to your own chair?"

She shook her head.

Chuck poured cereal into a bowl and sloshed milk over it.

Lyla picked up the spoon and scooped cereal into her mouth. With liquid dripping down her chin, she turned and gave him a milky smile.

"Whatever makes you happy." He sat while she finished her cereal, with Sid Sloth in the chair beside them.

"You two seem to be getting along rather well this morning."

Kate entered the kitchen, wearing jeans and a soft, baby-blue sweater. She was barefooted, and her hair was pulled back into a loose ponytail.

Chuck sucked air into his empty lungs. The woman took his breath away without even trying.

"I make a mean omelet," she said and bent to pull out of the cabinet the frying pan they'd purchased at the grocery store. When she straightened, her gaze met his. Her pupils flared, and her cheeks reddened.

She had to be remembering what they'd done in the living room the night before.

Chuck sure as hell was remembering.

Lyla set her spoon on the table, having finished her cereal. She raised her arms to Kate.

Kate set the pan on the stove and crossed the kitchen to lift Lyla into her arms.

Chuck cleared his throat. "Why don't you get in some morning cuddles while I fix breakfast."

Kate smiled down at Lyla. "You're on. Since I live on my own, I don't do a lot of cooking. No use cooking for one."

"I used to cook for my buddies on my SEAL team when we got together. Most of it involved a grill and huge amounts of steaks and ribs. But I've been known to make a decent breakfast when I have to."

She waved her hand. "I'm not arguing. By all means." Kate hugged Lyla close. "Where's Sid?"

"He's finishing his breakfast," Lyla said, pointing to the chair where Sid sat as if he were waiting for someone to serve him cereal and milk.

Chuckling softly, Chuck manned the stove, pulled out the carton of eggs, shredded cheese, green onions, bell peppers and tomatoes. He started bacon in the skillet, cooking it while he chopped the ingredients for the omelets.

By the time everything was ready, Lyla had moved into the living room by herself and was playing with Sid and the doll Sadie had sent.

"Need any help, or did I time that right?"

He smiled. "Sit. I'll serve."

"Yes, sir." She popped a sharp salute and took a seat at the little table.

Chuck set a plate full of a fluffy, yellow omelet and three slices of bacon in front of her.

"This looks amazing," she said and sniffed. "Smells even better. But I can't eat all of this. I'd be in a food coma before noon."

"You need to keep up your strength. We never know what to expect or when."

With her fork poised over the omelet, she stared up at him. "Do you think they'll find us here?"

"I don't know, but even if they don't, it doesn't hurt to be ready." He sat opposite her with a plate filled just like hers. "Eat up."

They ate breakfast together like a young married couple, talking and finding out more about each other.

"What does your boss think about you taking off for such a long period of time? Will you have a job to return to when Lyla and your sister are all settled?"

Kate smiled. "I should. I own the company."

Chuck leaned back. "I'm impressed."

She shrugged modestly. "I started out as a company of one employee. I now have twenty, and one of them is my general manager. She'll have everything under control. I've been handing the reins to her over the past year, ready to move on to another challenge."

"Like?"

Kate shrugged again. "I'm not sure. I haven't found anything that inspires me yet."

"The timing for relinquishing authority couldn't have been better, what with Lyla showing up on your doorstep."

"I know." She shook her head. "Some things can't be explained. You could say it was fate."

Chuck stared down at the food on his plate. "Fate can be benevolent at times, and sometimes she can be a bitch." He stabbed his fork into the omelet and raised a bite to his lips.

"Like when your family died in the car crash?" she asked softly.

He nodded. "And like finding Hank and the Brotherhood Protectors. I count myself lucky that I can use my training as a SEAL, taking care of others who might not be able to take care of themselves."

Kate nodded. "I'm just glad I could be here for Lyla. She's a beautiful little girl with a wonderful personality. I hope we can reunite her with her mother soon. I'm sure Rachel is beside herself worrying about her."

"Hank's working on finding her."

Kate set her fork down beside her plate. "I'm glad she knew to call on Hank and the brotherhood. I wouldn't have known which way to turn."

"Fate," Chuck concluded.

They finished their breakfast and laid out a plan to keep busy for the next few days. It included sprucing up the house with fresh paint on the interior walls.

After another trip to the hardware store for the supplies they needed, they spread plastic sheeting on the floors and furniture, opened the windows and went to work painting one room at a time.

For the next three days, Chuck kept his hands to himself, though it was a challenge.

The more time he spent with Kate and Lyla, the more he wanted to spend with them.

In the evenings, they sat around the living room. He or Kate read to Lyla, or Lyla played with Sid and the doll Sadie had given her.

Chuck insisted on cooking meals to keep from having to go out each night when Lyla was tired and cranky. Kate always pitched in, helping chop vegetables or setting the table. Lyla helped too, drying dishes and folding napkins.

An outsider looking in would think they were one happy family.

Even Chuck was beginning to feel that way. But he knew it couldn't last.

He touched base every day with Hank to keep abreast of anything Kujo found out about the cult in Idaho. So far, Kujo hadn't seen Rachel or made it past the cult's security. He'd reported that in order to get inside the camp, he'd have to join the cult. And the cult members weren't very open to outsiders at the time.

After the third day, they'd finished the painting inside by completing the touchup on the baseboards.

Three days inside was enough. Chuck cleaned the paintbrushes and washed his hands. "Who wants to go to the park?"

Lyla clapped her hands. "I do. I do."

Kate stood behind Lyla, her eyebrows pulling together. "You think it will be all right?"

Chuck nodded. "All three of us will go as a family."

Kate nodded and smiled. "Great! These walls were closing in, and the paint fumes are getting to me."

"We'll leave the windows open to air out the house. Ten minutes enough to wash the paint off the tip of your nose and change into clean clothes?"

Lyla ran for the bathroom.

Kate followed, touching the tip of her nose and looking down, cross-eyed, to see where the paint might be.

Chuck laughed, his heart light for the first time in what felt like years. He liked being with Kate and Lyla. If, at the end of this assignment, they parted ways, he would have at least learned something.

Life continued after losing a loved one. And he needed to live it.

With that in mind, he decided to enjoy the day while keeping a close watch on the two ladies in his care.

CHAPTER 9

KATE SCRUBBED the paint off her nose, hands and arms and helped Lyla do the same. After she helped her niece into clean clothing, she ran to her own room and dressed in freshly laundered jeans and a white, cotton blouse. She brushed her hair out and left it hanging long around her shoulders.

Chuck seemed to like it when she left her hair loose. His eyes darkened and his nostrils flared when she came into a room with her hair down around her shoulders.

For the past three days, she'd done her best to keep from begging him to make love to her again. And it was just as well she hadn't. Lyla had made a habit of waking up in the middle of the night calling out for her mama.

If she'd done that the first night in the house, the situation would have been embarrassing for all three of them and might have generated a barrage of questions Kate didn't want to have to provide the answers for.

Rachel should have that honor, several years down the road.

When Kate emerged from the bedroom, Chuck was attempting to teach Lyla how to play the Miss Mary Mack hand-clapping game in the living room.

Kate laughed when she saw them. "Where did you learn how to do that?"

A grin tipped up the corners of his mouth. "I have an older sister. She made me play this game until she had it down." He returned his attention to Lyla and tried again to get her to clap in the correct sequence. They both laughed.

Kate smiled at the silly game, but her smile faded as she remembered how she and Rachel had played that game and others when they were little girls, not much older than Lyla.

She wished Hank would find Rachel soon. She missed her sister and hoped she could help her out of whatever mess she'd landed in.

Chuck straightened, his gaze going to Kate. "Hank's people are on it. They'll find her," he said, as if reading her mind. "For now, we're going on a picnic to the park."

He lifted a backpack off the kitchen counter.

She blinked. "You made lunch that fast?"

"You ladies took more than ten minutes. I had plenty of time to make sandwiches and pack some chips, bottled water and a blanket."

"You're an amazing man." She cupped his cheek with her hand and leaned up to plant a kiss on his lips. She did it all as if it was the most natural thing to do. When she realized what she'd done, she shrugged. What the hell? Why not?

Without an apology, she swung her hair back over her shoulder and headed for the door. "Last one to the truck is a rotten egg."

She flung open the door and would have run out, but Chuck's hands caught her arm and Lyla's before either one could race outside.

That's when Kate noticed a man on the road outside the house, walking a dog.

He slowed as he passed the yellow cottage, his gaze swinging toward them, his eyes narrowing.

"I'm going to be a rotten egg," Lyla cried and wiggled free of Chuck's hand. She ran outside, straight for the truck.

Kate's heart stuttered, and then her pulse kicked into high speed. She ran after her, but Chuck reached her first, swinging her up into his arms. He carried her the last few steps to the truck and let her lean forward to touch the truck first.

"I win!" she called out.

"Yes, darlin', you win," Chuck said, his gaze on the man and dog. "Hop in so I can buckle your seat belt." Chuck opened the door and deposited Lyla on the seat, buckling her in and then closing the door firmly.

Kate stood beside him, trying not to be too obvious about watching the man walking his dog. She could see him in her peripheral vision. He'd walked to the end of the road, turned around and was on his way back.

"Hop in, sweetheart." Chuck held the passenger door for Kate. "He doesn't appear to be armed unless the dog is his weapon of choice. In which case, you need to get in."

Kate jumped up into the seat, and Chuck closed the door.

Her heart continued to race as Chuck rounded the truck and climbed into the driver's seat.

"Do you think he—" Kate broke off her sentence and nodded toward the stranger.

"I don't know, but apparently he's the one Mrs. Turner was talking about the other night."

"Should we stay at the house?"

"No. We're going on a picnic on the other side of town. Hopefully, he won't follow us there."

"And if he does?"

Chuck opened his jacket, displaying a shoulder holster with a handgun tucked inside.

Kate's eyes rounded briefly, but then she settled back in her seat, reassured he was prepared to protect them. As a SEAL, he had to be a good shot. She prayed he wouldn't have to use the gun, but she was glad he was packing.

The drive across town took less than five minutes, and only that long because they had to stop to let an old woman using a walker cross Main Street.

The sun was shining, the day was warm without being too hot and Kate was ready to breathe fresh air.

Yet she couldn't get over the feeling they were being watched. Perhaps it was seeing the man walking his dog that had set her on edge, but she had a hard time shaking the feeling.

At the park, they found a grassy spot beneath the

spreading branches of an oak tree and laid out their blanket.

They were only a few yards away from the playground equipment.

"I need to call Hank," Chuck said.

Lyla grabbed Kate's hand and dragged her toward the swing. "Push me. Please."

Kate looked over her head at Chuck. "It's not far. You can keep an eye on us while you talk to Hank." She nodded toward a woman who'd just arrived with her daughter. "Isn't that the woman from the grocery store?"

Chuck stared across the field at the woman as she and her daughter walked toward the swings. "I think so."

"We'll be fine. I'll stay close to Lyla. Join us when you're finished with your call."

"Okay, but don't go any farther."

"We won't."

"And Kate..." Chuck said.

"Yes?"

"Don't share information with anyone, no matter how inconsequential. Words have a way of finding the wrong ears."

"I'll be careful." Kate let Lyla lead her to the swings, while Chuck anchored the blanket with the backpack and pulled out his cellphone.

The woman she'd met in the grocery store was already at the swing set, gently pushing her daughter.

"Hello," Kate called out as she neared. "Becca and Mary, right?"

"That's right." The woman smiled. "And you're Kate and Lyla."

Kate nodded toward the woman and helped Lyla up into the swing. "Seems we keep running into each other."

"Hard not to, since it is such a small town."

"How are you settling in?" Kate asked, glad for a little variation in her adult conversation. Coming from a thriving marketing company in LA to being sequestered in a house with one man and one small child, she found she craved a little more social interaction.

"Actually, we're staying in a camper just outside of town while we look for just the right piece of property to buy." Becca pushed Mary in the swing in a steady rhythm. "We'd like to have a garden to grow our own vegetables."

"Wow. A camper?" Kate glanced around the park. "No wonder you're at the park. I'm sure the camper walls were closing in around you."

Becca nodded. "Yes, they were. It's nice to be outside in the fresh air. We needed the exercise."

Lyla looked back at Kate. "I want to climb on the slide."

"Okay, but be careful on the ladder." Kate stopped the swing.

Lyla jumped off and ran for the slide.

Becca stopped Mary and tipped her head toward the slide. "Why don't you go with Lyla and show her how it's done."

"Yes, ma'am," Mary said and hurried off to join Lyla.

Kate walked more sedately behind Lyla and found a bench within easy reach of Lyla and the slide. She sat on one end and was glad to see Becca settled onto the other end.

"Is Mary your only child?" Kate asked.

"No, I have two sons I left with my mother back where we're from. They're in school, and I didn't want to uproot them before we found a place to live."

"That's understandable." Kate glanced at Becca before turning back to watch Lyla. "It must be hard to be away from your children."

"It is, but they're used to being with my mother. She takes very good care of them."

Still, Kate couldn't imagine leaving even one of her children behind.

Her lips curled upward. Here she was thinking she wouldn't leave her children behind when she hadn't had any and probably never would. She was getting to that age when women had trouble getting pregnant. At the ripe old age of thirty-five, she'd resigned herself to being alone.

Until Lyla came into her life, and then Chuck.

The two of them had opened a door she thought completely closed. Now that she knew what she was missing...

Sweet heaven.

She wanted a family.

Her gaze went from Lyla to Chuck and back.

She'd always thought her life was perfect. She was a successful career woman with a nice apartment in an upscale area of LA. She had employees who looked up to her and clients who trusted her work and tastes. What more could she ask for?

A husband to come home to and a child to love.

Kate swallowed hard on the lump forming in her throat. She loved being with Lyla. Sure, she was a lot more work that she'd ever thought a three-year-old could be, but her niece gave the warmest, sweetest hugs. How could she not love that little girl? And Chuck… there was so much about the man that Kate could love. Her chest swelled, and her pulse quickened. God, she hoped their first night of passion wouldn't be their last.

He'd been her most amazing lover. But he was more than that. He'd more than proven his daddy skills, and he was fun to be with, smart and strong. He cared about the people around him and would do anything to protect them from harm.

After less than a week with Chuck, Kate could already tell she was falling for him. Hard.

"Are you and your husband settling in nicely?" Becca asked.

Kate frowned. "Did I say we were new in town?"

Becca shot a glance her way, and her cheeks reddened. "I don't remember. I just assumed you were new because you said you hadn't seen many children in town when we were back at the grocery store."

Kate remembered what Chuck had told her about sharing too much information with anybody. "Oh, we've been around for a while. I just meant that so many of our young couples leave town because there just aren't that many jobs in the area. Thus, fewer children Lyla's age."

Not that she considered Becca a threat, but what Becca shared with another stranger, might be that little bit of information an attacker could use to abscond with Lyla.

Kate wasn't taking any chances, but she wasn't going to be rude to the woman who only seemed to want a friend to talk with.

Mary and Lyla climbed the ladder and slid down the slide a number of times before they grew bored and climbed the monkey bars a few more steps away from where Kate sat.

Kate leaned forward, her gaze scanning the park for threats. So far, the park was empty, except for a man on the far side wearing a baseball cap and playing with a puppy.

He was far enough away, he wouldn't be a threat. Kate could reach Lyla before he could make it there.

She settled back and enjoyed the sunshine, her gaze again swinging from Lyla to Chuck and back. This was what life with the Navy SEAL could be like. If he was interested.

She cautioned herself not to raise her hopes too much. Just because he'd made love to her once, didn't mean he wanted to do it again. Hell, he hadn't made a move on her since.

Her lips twisted. Had making love to her been that bad?

CHUCK HELD the cellphone to his ear, trying to make out what Hank was talking about. The reception was spotty.

He'd done his best to give his boss an update, but he'd had to redial a couple of times already because of dropped calls.

He was most interested in learning more about Kujo's investigation of the cult community in Idaho.

"Kujo...into the camp...tight security," Hank was saying.

Chuck hated that he was only getting part of the conversation, and he had to ask for repeated clarification. "He got into the camp?"

"No. He couldn..."

"Has he seen Rachel?" Chuck asked.

"Not yet...and children seem to...guarded and...out of sight."

"Pretended to wander...the camp and... stopped before he...within a hundred yards."

Chuck snorted. "Why would they be that closed and have that good of security unless they were hiding something?"

"Or someone," Hank said.

"Exactly."

The phone went silent.

"Hank?" Chuck listened. Nothing. He looked down at his display only to find *Call Ended* written across the screen.

Muttering a curse, he dialed Hank's number again.

"The reception where you...is poor. Call me...cottage."

"Will do," Chuck said and ended the call. He'd spent more time than he cared to away from Lyla and Kate. And they had yet to partake of their picnic lunch.

He glanced toward Lyla who was playing on the monkey bars with Mary, the little girl they'd met at the grocery store.

His gaze went to Kate seated on a bench, not far from where Lyla was playing. She seemed content to chat with Becca while she watched Lyla play.

Anyone watching would think nothing of Kate watching her child play. She kept a close eye on Lyla, her glance rarely moving away from her niece. Then she leaned forward, her brow furrowing.

Chuck looked back toward Lyla, and he frowned.

Where she'd been a moment before, she was no longer. Then he saw both little girls running across the open field toward a man with a puppy.

Chuck was off like a rocket, running as fast as he could, pumping his arms and legs.

Lyla had a pretty good head start.

Kate was off the bench and well ahead of him, running for Lyla. She'd make it to her first.

The thing that had him scared was that Lyla could make it to the man and his puppy before Kate or Chuck could reach her.

His heart pounding and lungs burning, he ran fast, but not fast enough.

Lyla's little legs carried her across the grass and right up to the puppy.

The man stepped forward and leaned over the child, his hands outstretched.

"No!" Kate yelled. "Don't take her!"

Chuck caught up with Kate, passed her and dove for

Lyla just as the man's hand came in contact with the little girl.

With the grace of a hawk swooping in to claim his prey, Chuck snatched Lyla out of the clutches of the man and crushed her to his chest.

Kate came to a skidding stop in front of them, breathing hard, her hair in wild disarray around her face. "Is she all right?" she demanded between deep breaths of air.

"She's okay," Chuck said, his gaze on the man.

He'd scooped up the puppy and held it away from the small children, a frown creasing his forehead. "What the hell was that all about?" he asked.

"You were about to take my n—daughter," Kate said, a glare drawing her eyebrows into a V.

The man laughed. "No, your daughter was about to touch my puppy." He glanced down at the animal in his arms. "Duchess isn't used to small children. She might have bit your little girl. I was reaching down to rescue her."

Kate's frown deepened. "But I thought...and you were reaching...and I couldn't get..." She bent double and placed her hands on her knees, dragging in deep, ragged breaths. She waved toward Chuck. "Tell him."

"We thought you were trying to steal our little girl. Our mistake. Now, if you'll excuse us, we'll leave you alone."

Carrying Lyla in his arms, Chuck walked back toward the playground equipment.

Kate grabbed Mary's hand and led her back, following behind Chuck.

Becca met them halfway across the field. "What was that all about?"

"Nothing," Chuck said. "Just a misunderstanding."

"Mary, did you get to pet the puppy?" Becca asked.

"No, ma'am," she said and stood quietly next to her mother.

"Are you going to be here much longer?" Becca asked.

Chuck answered, "No. We have to be leaving. Remember that appointment we had?"

Kate glanced up at Chuck, her gaze questioning. But she nodded and played along. "Oh, yes. I almost forgot." She turned to Becca. "I enjoyed spending time with you and Mary. Perhaps we can do it again, soon."

"I'd like that, too. Will you be out tomorrow?" Becca asked, giving her a tentative smile.

"I'm not sure." Kate shot a glance toward Chuck.

His lips tightened. He hoped Kate picked up on his desire not to make plans. Set up times to be places could be used against them. An attacker could arrange to be there ahead of time and surprise them, make a grab for Lyla and be gone before they knew what had happened.

"I'll see you around," Kate finally said and hurried over to grab the blanket off the ground and swing the backpack over her shoulder.

They walked back to the truck in silence. Even Lyla was quiet.

Chuck buckled her in and held Kate's door for her while she climbed inside.

His heartbeat had barely settled back into a normal rhythm by the time he climbed into the driver's seat.

If the man with the puppy had decided to grab Lyla and make a run for it, he could have done it.

Kate and Chuck might not have gotten to her in time.

The whole situation made Chuck realize just how lax he'd gotten in his duty. He vowed to tighten up and take better care not to let his guard down for even a moment. Kate and Lyla were depending on him.

•

CHAPTER 10

KATE WAITED in the truck with Lyla while Chuck entered the house, checked it over thoroughly, and then returned with the all-clear sign of a thumbs-up.

She'd almost struck up a conversation a couple times on the short drive back to the cottage, but every time she glanced his way, his jaw was tight and his lips were pressed into a thin line.

Chuck appeared completely unapproachable and downright scary.

Instead, Kate clamped her lips together and waited for Chuck to loosen up. Apparently, Lyla running off to pet a puppy had rattled the SEAL. So much so, he had gone into professional bodyguard mode and was taking everything to the extreme.

Supper was the sandwiches Chuck had made.

Lyla pouted when they sat down at the dinner table. She was disappointed they hadn't had time to have a picnic in the park.

To make up for it, Kate spread the picnic blanket on the floor of the living room, and they ate their sandwiches, as if they were on a picnic.

Chuck even pretended an ant got on his sandwich, sending Lyla into a fit of the giggles.

By the time Kate's niece had her bath and dressed in her pajamas, she was already yawning.

Kate tucked her in, sat on the edge of her little bed and stroked her hair while reading from her favorite book.

Not three pages into the story, Lyla's eyes drifted closed.

Making her voice quieter and softer, Kate kept reading. When she was certain Lyla was fast asleep, she rose from the bed. She tucked Sid Sloth under the child's arm and dropped a kiss on her forehead. "Sleep tight, sweetheart. I love you."

Kate stared down at Lyla, wishing with all her heart her sister was okay and would be back soon to claim her daughter. When Rachel did come back, Kate would miss being Lyla's temporary mother. She'd miss reading stories to her and having picnics in the living room. She'd miss painting walls and eating hotdogs at the kitchen table. She'd miss being a family with Lyla and Chuck.

Her eyes blurring with unshed tears, Kate turned toward the door and stumbled into a hard wall of muscle.

Strong hands came up to cup her elbows. "What's wrong?"

Chuck's deep voice sounded so close to her ear, she

leaned toward it, blinking back the tears so that he wouldn't see them. "Nothing. I'm fine. Lyla's fine. We're all so freakin' fine."

Kate attempted to push past him, but he refused to release her arms.

"Seriously, what's got you all wound up?"

"Is it wrong for me to want my sister to come back but want her to stay away at the same time?" She swallowed back a sob and looked over her shoulder at Lyla. "I never thought I wanted children."

"Until you spent time with Lyla?" he said softly.

She nodded and a tear slipped from the corner of her eye. "Rachel had to be desperate to leave her. What could have gone so wrong that she would abandon that sweet little girl?" More tears spilled from her eyes. Tears she was helpless to contain.

Chuck tipped her chin up and pressed a kiss to her damp eyelids. "Rachel is going to be okay."

"I hope you're right." Kate sniffed. "And when she comes back for Lyla..." Her lips twisted, and the tears fell faster. "I'll miss her."

"Yeah. Me, too." Chuck pulled her into his arms and held her. "She has a way of fitting right into your heart, doesn't she?"

"Yes." Kate rested her cheek against Chuck's chest, listening to the reassuringly steady beat of his heart. She'd miss Chuck, too. How could two people have become so much a part of her life in such a short time?

Kate curled her fingers into the fabric of Chuck's shirt. She didn't want to let him go. Not now, not ever.

What was she thinking? She couldn't be in love with

the guy. Kate Phillips, marketing executive and career woman, couldn't possibly be in love with a man whom she'd only recently met. She'd never believed in love at first sight, or even insta-love. Relationships took time to build and grow. Didn't they?

"I don't know what I'm going to do," she whispered. "I don't want to let go."

Chuck brushed a strand of her hair back behind her ear. "You're a mess, you know that? For a woman who knew exactly what she wanted out of life, you're going all wishy-washy on me."

She laughed, the sound catching on a sob. "I know. It's not like me to lose it." Now, her tears were falling in earnest down her cheeks.

Chuck brushed away some of them with his thumbs, but there were too many to catch. "Darlin', you've got to shut off these waterworks, or you'll have me bawling before you know it."

Kate smiled at the thought and scrubbed at the tears on her cheeks. "I didn't think SEALs could cry."

"Oh, they can, all right. Just don't tell anyone. They'd never believe you anyway." He bent and scooped her up in his arms.

"Are you taking me to bed to make mad, passionate love to me?" She cupped his cheek in her hand. "Because, if you are, could you please hurry?"

He hesitated in the hallway, his glance going to the open door of her bedroom. Then he must have thought better of it because he turned the opposite direction. "Let's take this conversation to the living room. I can't think when you're naked."

She looped her arm around his neck as he carried her to the couch. "Do you mean that in a good way or a bad way?"

"Both." He sat on the couch and settled her across his lap.

"Are we going to talk? Or neck like teenagers?" She pressed her lips to his cheek. "You know where I want to go with it."

He cupped her cheeks between his palms and held her still. "Kate, what are we doing here?"

Her heart stilled for a second, and then thundered against the walls of her chest. "I thought it was pretty clear. Why else would you carry me here and sit with me in your lap." She frowned. "Am I getting mixed signals?" Kate wiggled on his lap, certain of a growing erection beneath her bottom.

"You're right. I had every intention of kissing you, but it's more than that. What are we doing? Where are we going?"

Her heart slid slowly into her gut, a bad feeling creeping through her soul. "I thought what we were feeling was mutual." She swallowed hard. "Is it not?"

Chuck nodded. "I can't deny that I have feelings for you. But I'm not sure where they're going."

"No?" Kate's voice choked into a whisper.

"I was married once. I had it all. A wife, a little girl much like Lyla, and a home to go to."

"And you lost it," Kate concluded softly. "I'm sorry you had to experience that. But that was years ago. You can't live forever in the past."

"No, but it's tainted my expectations for the future."

"I don't understand."

"What if I fall in love again?"

An icy blade stabbed Kate's heart. He'd said *if*.

Kate moved off his lap and sat on the couch beside him. "Go on," she encouraged, though she wasn't sure she wanted to hear what came next.

"What we've had this past week has been amazing. I feel like I'm a part of a family again. And frankly, it scares the hell out of me."

She frowned. "But you're a Navy SEAL. You've been in battles that would leave me quaking in fear. How can a family come close to that kind of trauma?"

He closed his eyes for a moment, before opening them again and giving her a bleak look. "I don't know if I could handle losing my family again. If I give my heart to someone and she dies, I don't think I could go on living."

Kate pushed up off the couch, and walked to the picture window and stared at the curtains drawn for the night. "So, what you're really saying is you don't want to commit to anyone, for fear of losing them."

"Yeah."

"I see." She turned to face him, pasting a smile on her face, though her heart was cracking into a million pieces. "And what happened the other night?"

"It was amazing. You're amazing." He stood and walked toward her, his arms outstretched as if to embrace her. "But it should never have happened."

Kate held up a hand and shook her head. "Stop."

"Kate, I don't want to hurt you."

"Who said you hurt me?" She lifted her chin and

widened her smile. "All of this week has been a big act for the sake of protecting Lyla. I don't expect anything else from you. The other night was just a bonus fling. Nothing more." She ducked around him and headed for the bedroom, her eyes stinging.

"Kate..." Chuck called out after her.

"I'm tired. I'm going to bed." At that point, she gave up trying to make a graceful exit and ran the rest of the way to the bedroom.

When she closed the door behind her, she leaned against it and slid to the floor, tears flowing silently down her cheeks.

What had she expected? A confirmed bachelor like Chuck wouldn't just fall for a career-minded, almost middle-aged woman. Not when he could have any woman on the planet with just the crook of his finger.

When he'd made love to her the other night, it had been sex. Not love. To think otherwise was setting herself up for a heaping helping of heartache.

Kate pressed a hand to her chest, the pain radiating throughout her body.

"Damn. Damn. Damn." She'd committed the ultimate folly and fallen in love with a man who couldn't love her in return. They wrote songs about it. Unrequited love. That would be the story of her life.

When Rachel returned to claim Lyla, Kate would go back to her life as a corporate executive. Back to her tastefully decorated apartment in LA and a life she thought she loved and had...until now.

She'd been a fool to start believing that the past few days they'd been acting as a family were real. They weren't. Everything had been an act to fool potential attackers. Only it had backfired.

Kate had begun to believe that fairytales really could come true.

She stared at the bed through her watery eyes, but couldn't drag herself up off the floor to get there. Instead, she lay down on the hardwood flooring and closed her eyes.

Maybe if she went to sleep, everything would be better in the morning. Chuck could have had second thoughts about never marrying or having children. They'd go on being a happy family— and pigs could learn to fly.

CHUCK PACED the living room floor, crossing the length in a few short strides then conducting an about-face and crossing again. Two, then three times, he caught himself short of marching down the hallway and pounding on Kate's door.

She had to understand where he was coming from. He couldn't open his heart again. It hurt way too much to lose someone you loved. The pain was worse than being shot and lasted so much longer.

He couldn't fall in love and risk losing everything all over again. But Kate made it easy to fall in love. Strong, capable and confident in herself, she was so very different from Anne. They weren't anything alike.

So, why couldn't he leave her alone? Why did he want to hold her, kiss her and make love to again and again? He knew he couldn't commit to a relationship.

Kate deserved a man who wasn't afraid of loving. A man who could give her the babies she now knew she wanted.

Chuck wasn't the man for her.

But the thought of any other man being with her, holding her in his arms, kissing and touching her intimately nearly brought Chuck to his knees.

How could he let her go into another man's life when he wanted her?

Holy hell. Was he falling in love with Kate?

He stared toward the door at the end of the hallway. Was that what had him running scared?

His head tried to tell him no, but his heart screamed yes!

The truth stared him straight in the eye. He'd fallen for Kate. Totally, completely and irreversibly. No amount of denying it could change that fact now.

Pushing her away had been a stupid defense mechanism he'd used on other women who'd tried to get close to him. The problem was that when he'd pushed her away, his heart went with her.

As if of their own accord, his feet carried him down the hallway to the master bedroom door. He lifted his hand to knock.

Before he could touch the wood-paneled door, pounding sounded on the front door in the living room.

He hesitated, knowing he had to undo the damage he'd just done or risk Kate walking away without giving him a second chance.

More pounding that had a desperation to it sounded. Chuck couldn't ignore it.

He gave one last glance at the door to the bedroom and ran for the front entrance.

"Chuck! Help!" cried a shaky female voice on the other side.

Chuck yanked open the door.

The elderly Mrs. Turner fell inside and into his arms. "Oh, please, help me."

"Mrs. Turner, what's wrong.

"My house—" She coughed and drew in a ragged breath. "My house is on fire and Geraldine is still inside!"

Even as she said the words, Chuck could smell the smoke.

"Kate!" he yelled. "Kate!"

Kate jerked open the door to the master bedroom, her hair in disarray, her eyes red-rimmed and puffy. When she saw Mrs. Turner, she hurried toward them. "What's happening?"

"My house is on fire, and Geraldine is still inside," Mrs. Turner wailed.

Chuck held onto Mrs. Turner's arms. "Who is Geraldine? A friend or relative?"

"No. She's my cat. Geraldine has been with me since my husband died. I can't lose her." The older woman pulled free of Chuck's hands. "I have to find her." She ran back out into the night.

Chuck shot a glance at Kate. "I have to help her."

"Go," she said. "I'll call 911 and stay here with Lyla."

"Lock the doors behind me and don't open for anyone but me." He reached for her and pulled her into his arms. "When I get back, we have to talk."

"No, we don't." Kate pulled back out of his grip. "You've said enough. I'm not dumb. I get it when I've been brushed off."

"No, Kate. I was wrong. Very wrong. But I can't do my apology justice until I make sure Mrs. Turner doesn't run into a burning house to save a cat."

"We'll be all right. Just go." Kate held open the door.

Chuck didn't want to leave her, but Mrs. Turner would go back into a burning building to save her cat if he didn't go after her and stop her.

"Wait." Kate ran to the kitchen, grabbed a dish towel and soaked it under the faucet. Quickly ringing it out, she handed it to him. "She can't run all that fast. You can catch her before she goes in."

"Thanks." He bent and brushed a quick kiss across her lips. "I was wrong, and you're amazing. We'll talk."

Then he ran out the door and across the yard to Mrs. Turner's house. Smoke leached out of the open windows and flames shone through the glass of one of the bedrooms.

The old woman was just reaching for the front doorknob.

"Mrs. Turner, wait!" he called out.

Mrs. Turner glanced back over her shoulder. "Geraldine."

"Don't go in," he shouted. "I will."

Mrs. Turner stood back as Chuck ran up the stairs.

He touched the doorknob with the tip of his finger. It wasn't hot, so he knew there wasn't much of a blaze yet in the living room. If the smoke and fire was only in the bedroom, he might have a chance to find the cat and get out before the whole house went up in flames.

"She's probably hiding under the couch or in the closet in my bedroom, the first door on your left down the hall," Mrs. Turner said. "She hides when she's scared."

Chuck opened the door and was immediately assailed with smoke.

He ducked low. "Promise me you'll stay out of the house, Mrs. Turner."

She nodded. "I promise."

"I'll do my best to find Geraldine." Chuck held the damp towel over his nose and entered the house, hunkering as low as he could to remain below the rising smoke.

Inside the house, the lights in the living room were still working. Apparently, the fire hadn't reached the breaker box or the lines connecting the house to the power pole.

He dropped to his knees and checked beneath the couch, feeling his way with his hands. Though he didn't encounter a furball, he felt dust bunnies and cat toys.

His eyes stung, but the towel helped to filter the smoke to keep him from breathing it into his lungs.

Chuck checked the kitchen as he passed and entered the hallway. Smoke poured out from beneath one of the bedroom doors. He touched the door handle to find it extremely hot. The sooner he got out of the house, the better. Old houses were tinderboxes that fed a fire. When the fire spread into the walls and attic, it would be all over.

Fortunately, the cat couldn't have gone into the bedroom with the closed door or it would likely have already died of smoke inhalation.

The first door on the left was open. Chuck pushed it wider and stepped inside. At first glance, he didn't see any sign of the cat. But then he didn't expect to. If the cat was in the bedroom, it would be under the bed or in the closet as Mrs. Turner had suggested.

The closet door was open as well with a clothes basket on the floor inside.

Though there were clothes in the basket, no cat was tangled amongst them.

Chuck pulled the basket out and searched the back of the closet and up on the shelf above.

No cat.

The smoke grew thicker, making his eyes burn and water. Even the damp cloth over his mouth and nose wasn't quite keeping him from breathing the thickening, tainted air.

Chuck dropped to his knees and crawled to the bed. The lights flickered and extinguished, leaving him feeling around in the dark.

He first encountered what felt like a plastic storage container. Dragging that out from beneath the bed, he touched on what felt like a suitcase.

The smoke was getting worse. He didn't have much time left before he had to get out. The roar and heat of the fire intensified. Over his head, flames penetrated the ceiling and large flakes of burning embers and ash fell down around his legs.

He scooted farther under the bed until he finally felt

something furry. Grabbing onto a leg, he dragged Geraldine toward him and was scratched for his efforts.

Refusing to release the leg he had, he pulled her closer, latched onto the scruff of her neck and inched backward until he cleared the bed.

Fire raged around him, smoke making it impossible to breathe. He covered his mouth with the damp cloth, inhaled as deeply as he could and wrapped the cloth around the cat's head and body and then dove for the door.

Just as he neared the threshold, the hallway ceiling crashed down, blocking his escape. He slammed shut the door and ran for the window.

When he tried to open it one-handed he couldn't get the window to budge and he couldn't put down the cat or it would go right back under the bed.

With time running out, he snatched a pillow off the bed, removed the pillow out of the case and shoved the cat into the pillowcase.

Quickly tying the opening in a knot, he set the cat on the floor, grabbed a vanity stool from near the dresser and bashed it against the window.

The old glass shattered.

Using the stool legs, he knocked the shards loose, tossed the cat in the pillowcase out on the grass and dove out just in time to breathe.

Behind him, the ceiling of the room he'd been in, crashed in, flames and sparks shooting out in a spray of fireworks.

Chuck sucked in air and coughed. Locating the pillowcase with the cat, he decided the cat was better off contained in the case. He lifted the cat, bag and all and rounded the front of the house.

Sirens screamed in the distance, and soon, the Eagle Rock Fire Department arrived in force.

Chuck located Mrs. Turner and handed her the cat in the bag. "Leave her in the bag for now or she might run away and get lost."

Mrs. Turner cried ugly tears as she clutched the smoke and soot-covered bag to her chest.

Inside, the cat yowled.

Chuck didn't care. He'd saved the woman's cat. Now, he had to get back to the little, yellow house and make sure the sparks from the Turner house didn't catch his home on fire.

CHAPTER 11

KATE STARED out the side window facing Mrs. Turner's house, her heart beating fast, worry making it impossible to settle down. She'd dressed in jeans and a sweatshirt and pulled on her shoes.

She had to be ready in case the fire spread from one house to the other. It hadn't rained the entire time she'd been in Eagle Rock, which meant the vegetation was dry and could catch fire from one of the many flying embers kicked up by the wind.

"Mama?" Lyla's voice sounded behind her.

Kate turned away from the devastation and held open her arms. "Hey, sweetie. Come here."

Lyla padded across the floor and into Kate's arms. "I couldn't sleep."

"Did you have another bad dream?" she asked and combed her fingers through her niece's hair. "I could read another book to you, if you like."

Lyla shook her head and looked over Kate's shoulder

to the window. "Is that a fire?"

Kate took her hand and held it in hers. "Yes, it is."

"Will the fire come here?"

"No, sweetie," Kate said, though she wasn't so sure herself. She'd be ready if it did. Getting Lyla to safety was her number one goal.

Pounding sounded on the door. "Police, open up! You need to evacuate, now."

Lyla squealed and buried her face in Kate's neck. "I'm scared."

"It's okay, honey. They just want us to get out in case the fire does spread. We're okay."

Lyla dared to lift her head. "Where's Daddy? I want Daddy Chuck."

Kate did, too.

More pounding sounded on the door. "Open up. You have to evacuate now," the voice called out.

Again, Lyla shrank against Kate.

Kate grabbed her purse from the counter and Lyla's blanket from the bedroom, and she ran for the door, carrying Lyla.

For a second, she hesitated. Chuck had warned her not to open the door for anyone but him. Surely he didn't expect her to ignore the police.

She unlocked the deadbolt and the lock on the knob. When she twisted the knob to open the door, it slammed inward, knocking her backward.

A man rushed in followed by a woman.

Kate didn't have time to think, nor the ability to defend herself with her hands full of Lyla. A cloth was shoved into her face, and she inhaled a sickly-sweet scent.

"Get the girl," the man said, his voice rough, urgent.

Kate's legs weakened, and she couldn't hold onto Lyla as someone yanked her from her arms.

"No, you can't take her," she mumbled, her vocal cords no longer hers to control as she slipped into the darkness and fell into the man's arms.

Her last coherent thought was of Chuck.

Please, help us.

THE EAGLE ROCK FIRE Chief waylaid Chuck as he crossed Mrs. Turner's yard, taking precious seconds of his time. He told the chief he'd be back to answer all his questions once he checked on his wife and daughter.

Chuck ran back to the little, yellow house and took the porch steps two at time, arriving at the front door.

His heart sank to the pit of his belly when he found the front door ajar. Without going inside, he knew.

Kate and Lyla were gone.

Inside, Kate's purse lay spilled across the floor, and Lyla's blanket lay beside it.

He raced through the little house, praying he was wrong but knowing the truth. When he returned to the front door, he had his cellphone out, dialing Hank.

Hank answered halfway through the first ring. "I was just about to jump in the truck. I heard on the police scanner that Old Lady Turner's house was on fire. Are you guys all right?"

His hand tightened on the phone. "I'm all right, but Kate and Lyla are gone."

"How?"

In a few abrupt sentences, Chuck explained about Mrs. Turner's cat and finding the door open, Kate's purse and Lyla's blanket.

"Any sign of forced entry?" Hank asked.

"No."

"Based on the purse and blanket, she opened the door, thinking she had to get out," Hank surmised.

Knowing he'd failed them, Chuck couldn't give up. He had to find them. "Where would they have taken them?"

"If Kate's still wearing the necklace I gave her, we can track her. Let me get Swede on it right now. And I'll be there in fifteen minutes—ten, if I own the road." Hank ended the call as abruptly as he'd answered.

Chuck left the house and returned to find Mrs. Turner sobbing in the arms of the fire chief.

When Chuck walked up, the chief took the opportunity to untangle himself from the older woman. "I have to check on a few things."

Mrs. Turner faced her house, tears slipping down her wrinkled cheeks. The fire had been extinguished, but the firefighters were still unloading gallons of water on the smoldering embers.

"Everything I own is gone. Everything. Including my husband's ashes."

"Mrs. Turner, you have Geraldine," Chuck reminded her.

She sniffed and hugged the cat still confined to the pillowcase. "Poor thing is beside herself."

As if on cue, the cat yowled a long, pained sound.

"If you need a place to stay, you can stay at our place," Chuck offered.

"I wouldn't dream of putting you out," Mrs. Turner said. "I can stay with Hugh and Greta or Wanda."

Chuck's jaw tightened. "You won't be putting us out. In fact, you'll have the place to yourself. Kate and Lyla had to leave. Family emergency."

Mrs. Turner touched his arm. "Oh, dear. I hope it isn't major."

"Me, too. We'll know more with time. For now, though, I have to leave as well. Work called. I have to go."

"You sure you won't mind if I stay in the house?"

"Not at all."

"Thank you. I'd rather be close by in case someone needs to ask me anything. And when they let me back into the wreckage, I hope to be able to salvage something. Anything." She sniffed and more tears slid down her tired face.

"I'm sure Kate wouldn't mind if you borrow some of her clothing. Help yourself to anything. I'll be back as soon as I can."

Hugh and Greta arrived a moment later, giving Chuck the chance to make his escape. He started toward Main Street and found a man walking his dog talking to a policeman.

"Excuse me," the man called out.

Chuck slowed, his eyes narrowing.

"Do you live in the yellow house?" the man asked.

"I do," Chuck replied.

"I've been trying to tell this officer that I saw something that worried me."

Chuck sucked in a breath and let it out slowly. "What did you see?"

"I'm new in town, but I like to walk my dog out here, because I can let Brutus off his leash to run and no one cares. I was at the end of the road when the shit hit the fan with the old lady's house." He waved toward the darkened end of the road. "Damned dog got a wild hair up his ass and chased off after a rabbit in the dark."

Chuck glanced over the man's shoulder toward Main Street, watching for Hank's truck. He wished the man would get to point.

"Anyway," the stranger continued. "I was back in the woods, trying to get Brutus back on his leash, when I heard the woman yelling. I got back to the road in time to see a man carrying a large sack over his shoulder, getting into a van. Then a woman carrying a crying child got into the van, and they drove away." He pointed toward the yellow cottage. "They came from that direction. I was afraid they were ransacking the house, but I wasn't there in time to stop them."

"Thank you for letting me know," Chuck stuck out his hand. "What's your name?"

The man shook his hand with a firm grip. "Lance Rankin." He nodded toward the police officer who had walked away. "I guess he's not interested in finding out if the house was looted."

"It wasn't, but the sack he was carrying was probably

my wife and the crying child was my daughter." Chuck spied Hank's truck. "Gotta go find them."

"Well, good luck, man. If you need anything, look me up. I'd be happy to help."

"Thanks."

"Semper Fi," Lance said.

Chuck did a double take. "Marine?"

Lance nodded. "Fresh out of the military. I'm here to look up a guy named Hank Patterson. I hear he might have some work for me. Want me to help get your wife back?"

"I'll let you know." Chuck didn't want to spend time with introductions to Hank. He'd get around to that after he found Kate and Lyla. He ran toward Main Street as Hank turned down the side street and eased to a stop behind all the emergency vehicles.

Chuck reached the truck before Hank could climb out and come looking for him.

"Good. I wasn't sure how to find you in that cluster." Hank backed out onto Main Street and headed out of town.

"Just talked to a marine who saw the people who took Kate and Lyla. They were in a van."

"Even better," Hank handed him a device with a green dot blinking on a screen. "Swede was able to get Kate's tracker to come up. We're following them."

Hank leaned forward in his seat. "Where are they going?"

"Looks like they're headed for Bozeman."

"Shouldn't we call the state police and have them head them off?"

Hank tightened his hands on the steering wheel. "I didn't have an idea of what kind of vehicle they might be in. Go ahead and call it in. Tell them to look for a van."

Chuck checked his cellphone and cursed. "No service."

"Want me to head back to town so that you can make that call?"

"How far ahead are they?"

Hank stared down at the device in Chuck's hand. "I'd say they have a fifteen-minute lead."

"You got any of your guys south of town or even in Bozeman?"

"Sorry. I have a call out to all of them, but they were assigned to outlying ranches providing security. Duke Morris is in Great Falls. His client owns a plane and offered to fly him into Bozeman in case we need him. Tate Parker is coming in from his ranch. I told him we were headed south and to get on the road toward Bozeman. He might catch up to us by the time we hit the city limits."

"That's four of us. You think whoever took Kate and Lyla will put up a fight?"

Hank's lips pressed into a tight line. "If they're from the same cult Kujo's been following, they might. He said the perimeter guards are armed with machine guns."

Chuck's gut tightened. "Let's hope we reach them before they get to Idaho."

Hank cast a sideways glance at Chuck. "We should be able to catch up to them well before that."

Thirty miles out of Bozeman, they'd made up at least

eight of the fifteen-minute lead Kate's captors had on them.

Hank shot a glance at the screen. "Uh-oh." He pulled up a GPS screen of Montana and enlarged the area.

Chuck tensed. "What?"

"Looks like they're headed for the airport in Three Forks."

"There's an airport at Three Forks?" Chuck asked, his heart thudding in his chest.

"A small one used mostly by general aviation flights."

"We're six minutes out." Hank laid his foot hard on the accelerator, pushing his truck past one hundred miles per hour. "Hold on."

Chuck clutched the armrest and prayed an elk or antelope didn't step out in front of the vehicle.

Rather than look at the road ahead, he studied the green blip on the screen. It had ceased moving. "They stopped." Hope rose in his chest. He stared at the dark road in front of the truck. Just a few more miles.

Hang in there, Kate and Lyla, he prayed.

Hank took the Three Forks exit and blew through town. The airport was southwest of the little burg. When it came in sight, Chuck could see the blinking light of a plane taking off into the sky.

"Please don't be them," he muttered beneath his breath. His gaze shifted back to the tracking device, and he let out a sigh of relief. The green blip hadn't moved.

They pulled up to the small airport.

Chuck pointed to a gray van parked near the gate. "There," he said. "The location device says she's in there."

Hank skidded to a stop behind the vehicle and both men jumped out.

Chuck pulled his handgun from the holster beneath his jacket and aimed it at the vehicle. "Cover me. I'm going in."

"Got your six," Hank reassured.

Chuck eased toward the van and around the side. The sliding door was open all the way, and the interior was empty.

Chuck cursed. "That plane that just left...I think they were on it." He leaned into the van and shined his cellphone flashlight at the interior. Something glinted beneath the beam.

Chuck pulled out the necklace with the tracking chip and clutched it in his palm. "They're on their own. We can't track them." He stared up into the sky, but the plane that had taken off was long gone, swallowed up by the indigo night sky.

Hank pulled out his cellphone. "I'm calling Kujo to give him the heads-up. Hopefully, that's where their abductors plan to go. If not, we have no way of locating them on the US continent."

Chuck pocketed the necklace and straightened, his heart in the vicinity of his knees, all hope fading. "What next, boss?"

"I'm going to reroute the plane Duke is in and have them land at this airport. We can fly out to just about anywhere. I'll get Swede on tracking the plane that left here. It must have a transponder code—unless they didn't file a flight plan and are flying without using instruments to guide them."

"And if Swede can't track them?"

"I'm putting a call into Kujo to stake out the closest airstrip to the cult community. If that's their destination, they might fly there."

"And where will we fly?" Chuck asked.

"Aiming for Idaho." Hank pulled out his cellphone and dialed. "My gut tells me that's where we'll find them." His attention turned to his cellphone. "Kujo, we have a problem I hope you can help us with."

Hank coordinated with Kujo and the other Brotherhood Protectors originally en route to Bozeman. Kujo would stake out the airport. Duke and Bear would meet them at the Three Forks Airport for pickup when the plane from Helena arrived.

Meanwhile, Chuck paced, wondering what was happening with Kate, praying they weren't on a wild goose chase to the wrong location. Kate and Lyla could be flying to Canada or Mexico, for all they knew. If they didn't locate them in the first forty-eight hours, they might never find them. Hell, they hadn't found Rachel and it had been almost a week since she'd disappeared.

Chuck walked faster, his steps taking him to the end of the taxiway. He turned and walked back in time to see Bear arrive.

Hank briefed them on the situation and had them meet at his truck. He opened the tool box to display an entire array of AR15s, similar to the M4A1 with SOPMOD upgrades used by members of DEVGRU. His stock also included handguns, Ka-Bar knives and ammunition.

Each man selected dark clothing, black armored

vests, helmets, night vision goggles and communications equipment, testing the radios as they waited for the plane to arrive. They packed the equipment in the go-bags Hank provided.

By the time they were ready, a plane touched down on the runway and taxied over to where they were waiting.

Steps were lowered and John Wayne "Duke" Morris stepped down and crossed the tarmac. "Thought we were landing in a cow pasture." He extended his hand to Hank. The two shook. "The pilot has instructions to take us anywhere we want to go, courtesy of Lena Love."

"The actress?" Bear asked. "You still covering her six?"

"Between Angel and I, we've got her covered."

"I thought she was a raging lunatic," Bear said.

"She is, but she trusts us to keep her from jumping off the deep end or someone shooting her because she's so hard to get along with." Duke chuckled. "We don't put up with her crap. I think she respects that."

"You sure you're still good for working with her?" Hank asked. "We don't need the business so much you have to put up with her orneriness."

"Don't worry." Duke waved a hand. "We have it covered. Besides the job has its perks. We're supposed to fly to St. Maarten Island in the Caribbean soon for a movie location shoot. That should be interesting."

The whole time they were talking, Hank was handing Duke the same equipment he'd outfitted Bear and Chuck with.

Duke weighed the AR15 in his hands. When he looked up, his eyebrows were high. "Are we expecting an all-out war?"

"We don't know what exactly to expect, but if we learn Kate and Lyla have been taken to the cult's location in Idaho, we have some intel. Kujo's been there on reconnaissance." Hank handed him a helmet and night vision goggles. "They've set up the perimeter with machine guns and loads of ammunition."

"Sounds like a friendly bunch. All on American soil. Go figure." He shook his head and helped himself to magazines full of ammunition for the rifle and handgun he selected.

Once Duke had all he needed, they loaded into the plane and the pilot set a course for the airstrip closest to where Kujo had been hanging out in the mountains of Idaho.

Normally, Chuck's gut was a reliable gauge of what was happening. But this time, all he could feel was cold dread. Perhaps he was too heavily invested in the outcome. Worst case scenario, the plane Kate and Lyla were on would crash. Much like the story of his wife and child. Or the team would get there too late to save Kate and Lyla from whatever horrific fate the cult had in store for them. Or they'd get there to discover Kate and Lyla weren't there at all and never were. They'd have to start their search all over. At least in the last scenario, they might have the chance of finding them alive.

Chuck forced himself to think positive. Kate and

Lyla were at the cult's camp. They'd swoop in and rescue them and Rachel.

He'd tell Kate he loved her. She'd tell him the same, and they'd live happily ever after.

A man had to have his dreams. Otherwise, life wasn't worth living.

CHAPTER 12

KATE CAME to with a splitting headache, her face lying against a cold, hard floor and darkness. She blinked her eyes several times just to make sure she was actually awake and not in some terrible nightmare.

Pain throbbed in her hip where it lay against the solid floor. She shifted and moaned.

Soft sobbing echoed against the walls, forcing Kate to go that extra little bit to full consciousness. "Hello," she called out.

The sobbing grew louder.

"Hey, who's there?" she called out, the hairs on the back of her neck standing at attention. The sobs sounded soft and feminine, but not childlike.

Child. Lyla!

Kate pushed to a sitting position. "Lyla?"

"She's not here," a voice said from a different direction. "I don't know where they took her."

Kate knew that voice. It sounded so much like hers. "Rachel?" Oh, dear, sweet Lord. "Rachel? It's you."

More sobs sounded from the other side of the room. Were there two women?

Kate ignored the sobs and felt her way across the floor until she bumped into another person. "Rachel?" Tears welled in her eyes and spilled down her face.

Rachel's cold arms wrapped around her. "Oh, Kate. They have Lyla." She shook with the force of her silent sobs. The woman in the other corner had the market on noisy crying.

"I tried to keep her safe," Kate said. "They tricked us by setting the house next door on fire."

"You did the best you could. I should have known I couldn't keep her safe. Once you're in their fold, they don't give up. They don't let go." Rachel hugged Kate, laying her head on Kate's shoulder. "I tried to make a run for it, but they found me. And now they have Lyla."

"We'll get her out of here. You'll see." Kate forced confidence into her voice. Though she wasn't sure how she'd make it happen, she would get Rachel and Lyla out of this hell.

"I tried to protect her. When they said she had to marry at eight years old, I knew we couldn't stay. They do horrible things to the women and young girls. I didn't see it at first. When I did, I begged Myles to leave. But he wouldn't listen. They brainwashed him. He became just like James."

"Who's James?" Kate asked.

"James Royce, the leader of the People of Ascension.

He says he's the voice of God." She cried into Kate's shirt. "What man of God preys on little girls?"

"None, sweetie." Kate smoothed a hand over Rachel's hair. "He's a monster."

"And that's why I had to leave."

Kate held her sister close, thankful they were finally together. If only the circumstances could have been different. "Why didn't you leave sooner?"

"I didn't know. They keep their secrets until you're assimilated into the cult. I just happened to take longer than the others. Myles and I lived on the outskirts in a log cabin. We grew our own food, taught Lyla to respect nature and I thought we had a good life. Until Myles was inducted into the inner circle. He changed. From the kind, gentle man and father of our child to an evil, horrible being willing to give over his own daughter to the leader as one of his wives."

Kate's heart lodged in her throat. "That's what they wanted? To make Lyla one of the leader's wives? She's only three years old."

"I know. At first, I thought it was just a way to protect her. James's wives and children are treated the best. They get the best food, the best lodging and clothing. The community shares the bounty of each family's harvest. But I never saw James's family contribute to the rest. When I asked why, I was beaten with a broomstick."

"Oh, Rachel. Why didn't you tell me what was going on?"

Rachel shrugged against her. "We barely talked anymore. Myles and I had already given up so many worldly things like television and telephones. When I could get to town and call you, I thought you wouldn't believe me if I told you what was going on. And I tried to convince Myles to leave and take our family somewhere far away from the madness."

"And what did he say?" Kate clenched her fists, already knowing it hadn't been good.

"He told James what I'd said. James gave him a leather strap and told him the only way to bring me in line was to beat the resistance out of me. I had to be taught what was expected." Rachel cried harder. "And he did. He beat me. Myles wasn't the sweet, kind man I married anymore. I couldn't stay. But I had no money, and I couldn't take much with me. All I could do was walk with Lyla out of the woods, all the way to a highway, where I hitched a ride with a kind, old trucker who took me all the way to California."

Kate's heart ached for her sister. All the while Rachel had been suffering, Kate had been living the life of a high-powered executive, with more money than she could ever spend. Shame made her heart heavy. "I'm so sorry, Rachel. I should have known. I should have been there for you."

Rachel shook her head. "You couldn't have known. I didn't tell you. I was afraid and ashamed of what I'd let happen. Running away seemed the only option. I don't know what would have happened if the truck driver hadn't been going my way. He even went as far as to give me enough money to take a taxi to your apartment, and he bought a stuffed animal for Lyla. I owe that man my life."

Kate smiled though her heart ached. So that's where Lyla had gotten Sid Sloth, perhaps her first and only stuffed animal. When they got out of the mess they were in, Auntie Kate was going to give that child all the stuffed animals she could ever want and to hell with James Royce.

The sobs grew louder from the woman in the corner.

"Who is she?" Kate asked.

"Margaret, one of the sister wives James grew tired of. When he no longer has a use for them, he kicks them out of his house, claiming they've sinned." Rachel snorted. "The only sin they've committed is being trapped in this hell."

"How long have you been here?" Kate asked.

"They caught me the day after I left Lyla with you. I've been here in this cell ever since."

"Oh, Rachel. I'm so sorry." Kate hugged her sister. "We're going to get out of here. I swear on my life. And we're going to get Lyla out as well. I love that little girl. She's amazing."

Rachel laughed, the sound breaking on a sob. "I've missed her so much. I tried hard to give her a normal life, despite James and his insanity. She deserves a chance to be a child. She deserves happiness."

"Yes, she does. And we're going to give it to her." Kate pushed to her feet. "Do they feed you and let you relieve yourself?"

Rachel let Kate pull her to her feet. "Twice a day they bring a meal. Once in the morning and again in the evening. We use a bucket in the other corner to relieve ourselves. Someone comes in once a day to empty it."

"Is it always dark in here?" Kate couldn't get over how pitch-black it was in the cell.

"When the sun comes up, we get a little light from beneath the doorway. Other than that, yes." Rachel sighed. "I've felt my way around the entire room. It's made of concrete blocks. I've even used the handle on the waste can to try and chink away at the grout, thinking I might dig my way out eventually. It's no use. This cell is escape-proof."

Kate's jaw hardened. "Nothing is escape-proof when people are involved." She reached for her sister again and hugged her close. "We have each other. You know we're stronger when we work together."

Rachel wrapped her arms around her sister and held on tight. "I'm sorry you got dragged into this mess, but I'm so glad you found me."

"Me, too." She set her sister to arm's length. "Rachel, they brought me in unconscious. Where exactly are we?"

"We're in the mountains of Idaho."

Hope swelled in Kate's chest, and she dropped her voice to a whisper. "I think we might get out of here sooner than you think."

"Really? How?"

"Do you remember telling me to go to Montana and find Hank Patterson?" The mere thought of the Brotherhood Protectors gave her courage. They would come. Chuck would be beside himself until he found them. Yes, he'd told her he didn't want a relationship. But the man was committed to his mission. He wouldn't stop until he found and freed them. Of that, Kate was absolutely certain.

Rachel squeezed her sister around her waist. "The truck driver told me that if I ever needed help from someone I could trust with my life, I should look up Hank Patterson in Montana. He said his son worked for him. He employs former military men and women. Did you find Hank?"

Kate laughed. "I did. And if I'm not mistaken, he and his guys will find us."

"Thank God." Rachel hugged her sister again. "I don't know if it's fate or divine intervention, but I think someone or something has a plan. We just have to learn what it is."

"Though Hank's guys will be coming, we can't wait for them to get here. We have to help ourselves and Lyla out of this situation." A plan formed in Kate's mind, and with that plan, confidence and a fierce determination returned. "For now, we should rest until daylight. We need to be ready when they bring in the morning food."

BY THE TIME they landed outside the small town of Angel's Rest, Idaho, the eastern sky had lightened with the gray of predawn.

The pilot offered to stay around for twenty-four hours to take them back to Eagle Rock when they were done with their business.

Hank thanked the man and led the way out of the plane onto the tarmac.

Kujo and his retired military working dog, Six, crossed from the fixed base operator's building where the general aviation planes were serviced. "You guys are a sight for sore eyes," Kujo said. He reached out and shook Hank's hand and then greeted the others as they descended from the plane, carrying their go-bags.

"What's the scoop?" Hank asked.

Kujo's brows drew together. "A plane landed here a couple of hours ago. A van, with several heavily armed men, met them on the tarmac. They offloaded their cargo and drove away. I followed them up into the hills. They were headed for the cult compound."

"Did you see what their cargo was?" Chuck held his breath, waiting for Kujo's response.

"No. I didn't want to get too close in case they saw me. But whatever it was took two people to load one of the bundles, and I think a woman loaded the other. I'm guessing it was the woman and child you thought it might be. The sizes looked about right. They must have given the woman something to knock her out. She wasn't struggling at all."

Chuck let go of the breath he'd been holding and pushed forward, his heart squeezing so hard it hurt. "Take us to the camp."

"It'll be daylight by the time we get there," Kujo warned. "We'll need to move in slowly. They have a pretty tight perimeter, and they mean business. They're fortified with manned machine guns and men armed with semi-automatic rifles."

"Think they know how to use them?" Hank asked.

Kujo nodded. "I know they do. I found where they

practice. It looked like something mocked-up for military training in urban terrain. These guys are badass."

Hank frowned. "Then we have to tread lightly. We're not in a war zone. We're on American soil. If they own the land, they might have the right to defend it." He glanced around at the men. "Number one...don't kill anyone, unless it's your last choice. Number two...be careful, there might be collateral damage if anyone starts shooting."

"And there would be." Kujo's mouth set in a grim line. "Inside the perimeter is an entire community with women and children."

"Which means, we can't go in shooting everything that moves," Hank said. "Killing women and children isn't what we do."

"And it's bad for business," Kujo agreed.

"What *do* we have going for us?" Duke asked.

"Someone inside that compound kidnapped two women and a child," Chuck said.

Hank nodded. "Those people are on the wrong side of the law. We're only going in to rescue our clients."

They followed Kujo to the large SUV he'd rented for his stay in Angel's Rest, and loaded their gear in the rear and then climbed inside, filling all the seats.

Six lay on the floor between the captain's chairs and rested his head on his paws.

The ride up into the mountains would have been nice if Chuck wasn't worried about Kate, Lyla and Rachel. The road wound through national forests, across rivers and past stark bluffs. The soft morning sun shone through the canopy of leaves, giving a false sense of peace in a place sure to test their abilities.

Eventually, they turned off the paved highway and bumped along a dirt road for another couple of miles.

"I found this road while out hiking the area. It parallels the one leading into the cult compound," Kujo said. "It's not as well maintained, but it serves the purpose of getting us closer without having to walk several more miles unnecessarily."

He tipped his head toward a cooler on the back seat. "There are sandwiches and drinks in the cooler. You might want to fuel up before we start our hike. The hills are steep and rocky. It'll take some time getting in. If we play our cards right, we can get close enough that I can show you where the perimeter guards are located before dark. Then when night falls, we can sneak past them or take them out. Either way, we'll get in."

Chuck wasn't hungry, but he ate anyway. He understood the necessity of providing his body with fuel. If he wasn't in top physical condition, he put his teammates at risk. So, he ate a sandwich, wondering if Kate and Lyla's captors were feeding them so that they could keep up their strength.

He hated that Kate had been kidnapped and hated even worse that Lyla had been subjected to this nightmare yet again. At this rate, the poor kid would have bad dreams for the rest of her life.

He vowed to find the three of them and get them out unscathed. Failure wasn't an option.

Kujo parked the SUV beneath the spreading branches of an oak tree.

The men climbed out, donned their gear and performed a comm check with their radios. When everyone was ready, they moved swiftly through the woods while they could. Kujo explained that once they crossed over a certain ridge, they'd have to slow down and move carefully to avoid detection.

Chuck had to resist the urge to charge through the woods and right into the camp. He would be of no help to the women if the perimeter guards shot him and left him for dead.

The men spread out, using the skills they'd attained while training with special operations teams. Noise discipline was fully enforced. Along the way, they gathered additional leaves and foliage to camouflage their helmets and clothing.

Kujo led the way, pausing at the top of a ridge to point out where they were heading and the location of the cult's camp. "From here on, move slowly, deliberately and keep low. They're using real bullets in those machine guns and rifles."

Hank waved his hand indicating they should move out.

One by one, they slipped over the top of the ridge and descended into a broad valley.

In the distance, Chuck could make out a few buildings and a farm field. As they dropped lower, climbing over rocks and boulders, he lost sight of the village, but he knew about how far it was and hope built in his chest. He had a hard time slowing down when he wanted to race ahead, find his girls and get them out of harm's way.

But he followed Kujo's lead. The man had spent time spying on the closed community. He would know what they had to do in order to stay safe, get past the perimeter guards and rescue the women.

By the time Kujo brought them to a halt, it was past noon.

Though the air in the mountains was still a bit chilly, Chuck had worked up a sweat, climbing over hills and easing past some rugged obstacles.

"We stop here," Kujo said into Chuck's headset. "The guard manning the machine gun is at our ten-o'clock position. Look closely. He's using camouflage netting to blend into his surroundings, only the camouflage is lighter than the surrounding green of the trees. Do you see it?"

A moment of silence passed.

"I see him," Duke acknowledged.

"Me, too," Hank said.

Chuck raised his mini binoculars and studied the terrain until he too spotted the camouflage netting. "I see him."

"Got 'em," Bear chimed in.

"Now," Kujo said. "Look toward the two-o'clock position. There's a man sleeping at his post. He's armed with a semi-automatic rifle."

Once again, the men chimed in when they spotted the second guard.

"There are three more positions in the woods and a pair of guards on the road leading into the community." Kujo had done well with his recon mission.

"We can't see anything of the community from here?" Hank said.

"No, you have to get past the perimeter guards to get close enough to see what's going on in the village," Kujo admitted. "I was able to sneak past the two guards on the northern end of the perimeter a couple of times. But other than the training they're conducting, I didn't see much else. They have gardens they tend and fields of wheat and corn. They farm using mules and primitive plows. "

"Kate, Lyla and Rachel have to be in there somewhere," Chuck said.

"Most of the buildings are made of logs cut from the surrounding forest. But there is one larger structure made of concrete blocks, located in the center of the community," Kujo said. "I didn't see a whole lot of movement around it, but that would be my bet if they're being held captive."

"That's our objective," Hank said. "We'll wait until nightfall to enter the camp. By then, the women and children will be inside, eating their evening meal or in bed and sleeping. For now, rest in place. We move as soon as it gets dark."

Chuck stared at the woods ahead, every muscle in his body tense, ready to rush into the village and free the woman he'd fallen head over heels for. Love? Yes, he loved her. Was it too soon to know? Hell, no.

Why else would he feel so horrible? If he didn't care about her, he might not be so anxious to get this extraction operation under way.

He lay on the ground, his weapon pointed toward

the machine gun nest. Drawing on his experience as a SEAL, he focused on controlling his respiration and heart rate. If he didn't relax and let his body rest, he'd be worn out before he took one step toward the camp. At the ripe old age of forty-seven, he worked out, ran and lifted weights. But he knew enough to recognize that he had to pace himself.

Chuck lay still, his pulse slowing, his breathing becoming more regular. He had a mission to accomplish, and he needed every bit of strength and stamina to do it right.

When the sun dipped over the edge of the western ridgeline, the lengthening shadows blended into the dark gray of dusk.

They'd be moving soon. It wouldn't be long before he would be reunited with Kate and Lyla. He could barely wait another minute to see them, but he practiced patience, praying they were all right and everything would turn out okay. He sure as hell couldn't lose them now. Not when his heart was fully committed to the love he felt.

"Time to move out," Hank said into Chuck's headset.

He gave his full focus to the mission ahead, and set out to do it to the best of his abilities. Lives depended on him. Lyla's, Rachel's and Kate's lives.

CHAPTER 13

KATE WAITED through the day for someone to open the door to their cell. But no one came. Her stomach rumbled and by the fading light beneath the door, she guessed the sun was setting. And still, no one came to give them food or water.

"This is the first time they've skipped feeding us breakfast," Rachel said.

In the limited light, Kate studied her sister. Her skin was pale, except where shadows made dark crescents beneath her eyes. She'd lost weight since Kate had last seen her, appearing almost gaunt.

When they got out of there, Kate was going to feed her sister good food and take care of her. She'd never have to be afraid again.

First, they had to get out of their prison.

Darkness claimed the cell again. Night settled in. Hunger knifed through her belly, but Kate refused to let it bring her down. She hadn't been there as long as Rachel. One day without food wouldn't slow her.

Footsteps sounded outside the metal door of their prison, and keys rattled and scraped against the lock.

The door opened, and a woman entered carrying a tray of food.

A man stood behind her, holding a lantern.

Kate recognized the woman as Becca, the lady who, with her daughter Mary, had befriended her in the park in Eagle Rock. "Becca?"

Becca cast her eyes downward. "You should eat," she said softly.

"You were part of bringing me and Lyla here?" Kate shook her head. "Why?"

"It's not for me to explain. I only do as my husband commands," she said and slid her eyes sideways as if motioning toward the man with the lantern. Her husband, Daniel.

Anger burned in Kate's gut. "You lied to me and took my child."

"She was not yours to take," the man said from the doorway. "The child belongs to the collective."

"She doesn't belong to the collective." Kate's hands balled into fists. "She should be with her mother."

"Please," Becca begged. "Take the tray. You need to eat to keep up your strength."

Clearly, the woman was cowed by the man behind her. This made Kate even angrier. But she held her temper in check, channeling it into a plan.

She took the tray from Becca and then tipped it. The food slipped onto the floor.

"Oh, now look what you've done." Becca ducked to pick up what she could, leaving a clear line from Kate to the man in the doorway.

Curling her arm, Kate flung the tray like a frisbee, aiming it at Daniel's throat. Her aim was true. The tray slammed into the man's Adam's apple. He dropped the lantern. The lantern oil spilled onto his jeans, and the flame caught his pant leg on fire.

Daniel clutched at his throat, gasping for breath while the flames climbed up his leg.

Kate grabbed Rachel's hand and ran for the door.

Blocking her path, Daniel hopped up and down in an attempt to put out the fire.

Once again, Kate put her kickboxing class to use and planted her heel in Daniel's gut, knocking him backward. His head hit the concrete wall with a loud thud, and he slid to the ground.

"Run!" Holding Rachel's hand, Kate dashed past Daniel and ran for a set of stairs.

"Wait," a voice called out behind them. "Take me with you."

Kate paused with her foot on the bottom step and glanced back at Becca, her hands outstretched.

As Becca passed her husband, Daniel reached out and snagged her ankle. She fell hard, landing on her stomach.

Daniel raised his fist to punch her.

Kate ran back and kicked his arm before he could land the punch.

He roared, rolled to the side and lurched to his feet,

towering over Kate. "I should have killed you instead of bringing you here."

Kate crouched in a fighting position, her eyes narrowing. "You're not going to do either."

The big man's face glowed a ruddy red in his anger. He seemed to have forgotten the fire climbing up his leg, burning his skin.

Kate cocked her leg and hit him in the kneecap.

Daniel clenched his fist and swung hard.

Kate ducked but not fast enough.

His fist clipped the top of her head, sending her staggering backward.

"Kate!" Rachel cried.

Before Kate's vision could clear, Daniel swung again.

Only this time, his fist didn't make it to her face.

Becca had swung the lantern, catching Daniel's arm, blocking the blow meant for Kate. Oil spilled out of the crushed lantern onto Daniel's arm, and his shirt burst into flames.

The man screamed and staggered backward.

Becca grabbed Margaret's arm and dragged her out of the cell.

The four women raced up the steps and out into the open, night air.

"Where are your children?" Kate demanded.

"In James's house," Becca said. "But you won't get inside. He has guards."

"We're getting inside," Kate vowed. "I'm not leaving Lyla with that lunatic. Show me the way."

Becca backed up several steps. "I c-can't."

"You can, and you will." Kate snagged the woman's arm. "Show me. I'll do the rest."

Margaret stepped forward. "I'll show you the back way into the house. I lived there for seven years. I know how to get in and out without being seen." She darted a glance left then right. "Follow me." Then she slipped into the shadows cast by the stars lighting up the sky.

"Stay and risk being caught, or come with us," Kate said to Becca. "We're going after Lyla and Mary."

Becca bit her lip, her eyes wide with fear. "You don't know what he's like."

"We're going." Kate left Becca standing in the doorway of the camp prison. A moment later, she heard the sound of footsteps behind her. Becca hurried to catch up.

Margaret had the lead, slipping from shadow to shadow alongside the buildings lining the road through the village. At the northern end of the village stood a much larger building made of stone and cedar, not the rustic log cabins so many had built with their bare hands and lived in with nothing more than wood-burning heat.

Margaret skirted the front of the building and scurried around to the back.

Kate paused between buildings and gripped her sister's arms. "Stay here. There's no need for both of us to go in. I'll get Lyla out. If anything happens to me, get out of the camp and find help."

"Kate, I can't let you go in there alone," Rachel said. "You don't understand. James is…" she shook her head. "He's evil. He's charismatic, charming when he wants to be, and he makes you believe what he wants you to believe."

"I won't fall for his nonsense," Kate promised.

"I didn't think I would either, but I watched so many others caught in his spell, and I was too."

"I'm not one of them, Rachel. And you aren't either, not anymore. You got out once. You'll get out again. Now, wait here and be ready to go for help if I don't come out with Lyla in the next five minutes. Got it?"

Rachel hugged Kate hard and let her go. "I love you, sister."

"I love you, too." Kate left Rachel hiding in the shadows.

CHUCK TOOK point on neutralizing the machine gun. He slipped through the night, placing each foot carefully to avoid making a sound.

Circling wide, he came from the rear of the machine gun nest, dropped into the fox hole and grabbed the man from behind in a choke hold.

Fortunately, the gunner hadn't had his finger on the trigger. He struggled but was no match for Chuck's superior strength. When the man went limp in Chuck's arms, he lowered him to the ground, checked quickly for a pulse and then secured him with zip ties. He slapped duct tape over the man's mouth and left him lying in the foxhole.

"Machine gun neutralized," he informed the others.

"Got my rifleman," Duke reported.

"Should we take out the others?" Bear asked.

"No time. We need to keep moving," Hank said. "If they check in with the perimeter guards and find the ones we tied up, they'll set off an alarm. Things will get sticky."

The men moved through the night, easing into the little village.

Kujo led the way to the cinder-block building.

Chuck followed as close as he could, covering his teammate's six.

Although it had been years since he'd been on a mission working with a team, his training came back to him. Once they were in the village proper, Chuck covered while Kujo moved forward. Then Kujo covered him while Chuck moved forward.

They didn't know what to expect in the way of resistance inside the camp. The occupants might consider themselves sufficiently protected with the perimeter guards and the two on the road leading in. Then again, they might have snipers perched on the rooftops of the log cabins.

Chuck doubted that, but then he wasn't willing to put it to the test. He covered Kujo as if snipers were waiting to pick them off, one by one.

Hank, Duke and Bear followed Chuck, leap-frogging their way from building to building.

Chuck made it to the concrete-block building first. The entrance door stood open with a set of stairs leading downward.

He paused long enough to shift his night vision goggles into place. A giant green blob of a human staggered out of the darkness, cursing. "That damned woman. I'll kill her."

Shifting the goggles back up on his helmet, Chuck stepped through the door, closed it behind him and switched on the flashlight clipped to his vest, shining it right into the eyes of the man threating to murder a woman.

That's when he recognized him. This was the same man he and Kate had run into in the grocery store in Eagle Rock. "Where's Kate?" Chuck asked in a low and dangerous voice. He dropped down a step. "I'll give you two seconds to answer, which is more than you gave her before kidnapping her."

"I don't know where the bitch went." His lip curled up in a snarl. "She won't get out of camp. No one does."

"That's where you're wrong." Chuck descended another step. "Time's up." As he rushed down the rest of the stairs, Daniel roared and ran up.

They met like clashing Titans.

Though Daniel was younger, he didn't have the same set of battle skills as Chuck. With minimal effort, Chuck twisted the man's arm up behind his back and pinned him face-first against the wall. "Where's Kate?" He shoved the man's arm higher up the middle of his back.

Daniel cried out. "I don't know. She kicked me in the gut and ran out of here with three other women."

The door at the top of the stairs opened. "Everything all right?" Kujo whispered into Chuck's headset.

"They were in here," Chuck said. "If you'll give me a hand…"

Kujo hurried down the stairs.

Chuck made quick work of binding the man's wrists with a zip tie and then his ankles.

Kujo covered his mouth with duct tape.

Leaving Daniel at the bottom of the stairs, Chuck and Kujo stepped out of the building.

"Where to now?" Chuck asked.

"Chuck, Kujo, head north. We found two women hiding in the shadows. One says she's Kate's sister, Rachel."

Chuck resisted the urge to race up the road. Instead, he and Kujo covered each other as they slipped from shadow to shadow until they joined the other three Brotherhood Protectors.

A woman who looked a lot like Kate shivered in the shadows with the woman Chuck recognized as Becca, Daniel's wife.

Chuck's fists clenched. "What have you done with Kate?" he demanded in a hushed tone.

Becca held up her hands. "I helped her escape," she said.

"The hell you did." Chuck fought to keep from wrapping his hands around the woman's neck. "You and your husband helped kidnap her and Lyla."

"I had to," she said. Her chin dipped to her chest. "My husband made me. If I didn't help, he would have beat me and my daughter."

Chuck didn't want to believe her, but after meeting Daniel...He tightened his lips. "Where's Kate?"

"She went after Lyla." Rachel stepped forward and pointed. "She's in that building."

The men studied the rock and cedar structure.

"It belongs to the cult leader, James Royce." Rachel's voice shook. Her teeth chattered in the cool night air. "He has Lyla and Mary. Kate made me promise to find help if she wasn't out in five minutes." She stared into Chuck's gaze. "She's been in there longer than five minutes." A sob choked her last words. "Please, help her."

CHAPTER 14

KATE AND MARGARET slipped through a gate in the walled garden at the rear of James Royce's house.

"They lock the back door every night, but I can pick the lock," Margaret said.

Following the woman, Kate weaved her way through a garden of vegetables and flowers to a door half-hidden by a rose trellis.

The scent of roses filling the air was incongruous with the terror constricting Kate's lungs.

She pushed past the fear, knowing she might be Lyla's only hope of escape. Yes, the men of Hank's brotherhood would be there soon. She had no doubt of that. But she couldn't risk James taking Lyla hostage or making a run for it, taking the child along as his insurance policy.

Kate had to get to the little girl before James realized the women had escaped, and before the former special operations guys converged on the complex.

Margaret reached the door first and felt about the doorframe with her hand. She retrieved a narrow metal file and stuck it into the lock on the doorknob.

With a few quick jiggles, she unlocked the door and pushed it open. Pressing a finger to her lips, she led the way into the house and down a long corridor.

The doors on either side opened outward and had padlocks on the outside.

A chill raced across Kate's skin. What kind of monster locked the people of his household inside their rooms? What if there was a fire? They'd all perish before anyone could get them out.

Even more determined to find Lyla, Kate pushed forward with Margaret leading the way.

The hallway ended in a large, starkly-furnished living area. The floor was made of stone tiles with no soft rugs for bare feet to walk on.

There wasn't a speck of dust or dirt anywhere to be seen. The area barely appeared to be lived in.

Margaret turned and walked along the wall to another hallway much like the first. She stopped halfway down that hall and used her file to pick the padlock hanging on the hasp.

The lock clicked, echoing loudly in the quiet corridor.

"What are you doing here?" a woman's voice called out from behind Kate and Margaret.

Margaret pulled off the lock and turned to face the woman. She pushed Kate behind her and whispered. "Find your girl." Louder she said, "I came back for my son."

"He is no longer your son," the woman said. "You were cast out of this household. Your children belong to James."

"No," Margaret said. "I will not abandon my children. They belong with me."

Kate fumbled with the door handle and pulled hard. The door didn't open. Glancing upward, she noted a latch. She reached up and flipped the latch over then jerked open the door. "Lyla?" she called out. "Mary."

"Mama?" a little voice responded. The five-year-old Kate had met at the park rose from a pallet of blankets on the floor.

"Mary, come with me, now." She rushed in, grabbed Mary's hand and led her toward the door.

Half a dozen little heads lifted from their pallets. All eyes looked toward Kate. They were all little children, probably no more than five years old. Kate's heart pinched hard in her chest. And none of them were her niece. She turned to Mary. "Where's Lyla?"

"He took her." Mary's face scrunched, and tears welled in her eyes. "I want my mama."

"Who took her?" Kate asked. In her gut, she already knew.

"Our father," Mary said, tears rolling down her cheeks. "Please. I want my mama."

The other children in the room heard Mary crying, and started crying too.

Kate hated leaving them, but she had to find Lyla before James did something stupid.

She backed out of the room to find Margaret

pressed against the wall by a woman twice her size and a man standing nearby, holding Lyla in his arms.

Kate straightened with Mary's hand in hers. "Let Lyla go, James. She's done nothing to hurt you."

"Mama," Lyla called out and leaned toward her with arms outstretched.

James tightened his hold on the little girl. "Quiet!" he thundered, his eyes narrowing. "I value each of my children. They are the future. I will not allow them to be poisoned by the heathens existing outside our paradise."

Kate snorted. "Paradise? What kind of paradise forces its residents to stay when they want to leave? What kind of paradise locks its people in at night?"

"They are locked in for their protection."

"Against whom?" Kate demanded. "The only person I see who poses a threat is you."

He raised a finger and pointed. "You are a pariah. You know not of what you speak."

"Oh, cut the preacher crap. You don't impress me. A man who threatens women and children isn't a man at all. He's a coward who can only control those who are weaker." Kate let go of Mary's hand and eased past the woman holding Margaret hostage.

One rescue at a time. Lyla needed her.

"Let go of the child," Kate reiterated, her voice dropping to a low, menacing warning.

"Or what?" James cocked an eyebrow. "It appears I'm the only one with anything to bargain with." He tipped his head toward Lyla, who was crying softly in his arms. "If I like, I could snap her neck before you reach me. Is that what you want?" He asked like he was inquiring what flavor of ice cream she preferred. Then his tone grew deeper and his lips pulled back in a feral snarl. "Because if you come one step closer, that's what I'll do."

Kate stopped five feet short of where James stood with Lyla. The man was insane. She wouldn't put it past him to hurt Lyla.

"Just put Lyla down. Take me in her place. She's just a little girl."

"Mama," Lyla cried. She wiggled and slipped free of his grip. Sliding down the man's body.

James grabbed at air, unable to catch her.

Lyla landed on her feet and darted toward Kate.

James dove after her, grabbing her by the hair.

Rage ripped through Kate, and she lunged for James, plowing into him headfirst.

When Kate hit him in the gut, he released Lyla's hair as he flew backward and slammed against the wall.

Kate yelled, "Run, Lyla!"

James grabbed Kate around the waist, rolled her over and straddled her back. "You have been nothing but trouble since you and Myles came. I should have done away with you when I did away with Myles." He gripped a handful of her hair and pulled back her head. "If you aren't a believer, you're done."

Kate was pinned to the ground with no way to fight back. She closed her eyes, prepared for the man to slam her head against the hard stone floor. Her head would crack open like a melon. "James, don't," she said, her voice raspy, her throat stretched with the force of him pulling her backward.

"What you don't understand is that I do as I please. I'm the messenger of God."

"Not anymore, you're not," a deep voice rumbled off the walls. The weight on Kate's back lifted, but the hand in her hair dragged her up with it.

Kate's heart filled with joy. Chuck had found them.

"Let go of her," Chuck commanded.

"No." Royce's voice was nothing more than a gasp.

"Do it, or I'll snap your neck like you threatened to snap Lyla's."

Kate couldn't see behind her, but she could tell Chuck had a hold of Royce and was hurting him.

Eventually, the man released his hold on Kate's hair.

She dropped to her knees and crawled forward. Once she was well out of his reach, she leaped to her feet.

Chuck had Royce in a chokehold, his face set in grim lines. "Nobody threatens my family," he said, his voice a low growl. "Do you understand?"

Kate's heart thudded dully. She'd never seen that look on Chuck's face.

Royce could only nod, his face turning red and then blue from lack of oxygen.

"He's not worth it, Chuck." Hank entered the hallway behind Chuck. "I have the state police on their way. This man is going to jail for the rest of his life. He deserves to die there."

Still, Chuck refused to release the man.

Kate touched his arm. "Chuck. Let him go. He can't hurt us anymore."

Chuck stared down into Kate's eyes. "He would have killed you."

"But he didn't." She smiled, although her scalp still hurt from how hard Royce had pulled her hair.

Lyla ran to her and wrapped her little arms around her legs.

Kate lifted her up and hugged her tight. "We're okay. Let him go."

Finally, Chuck relinquished his hold to Kujo who bound the man's wrists with zip ties and led him out of the building into the night.

Margaret stood beside Hank. The woman who'd held her captive sat on the ground, her face buried in her hands. Her wrists were bound in front of her.

"Give Margaret the keys," Kate commanded of the woman.

The woman unhooked a huge ring of keys from a belt around her waist, and handed them to Margaret.

Margaret went from room to room, unlocking the padlocks. Duke and Bear helped. Soon, all the women and children were freed, many of them crying, not knowing what was happening or what would happen to them now that they weren't under James Royce's control.

Chuck took Lyla in his arms and wrapped his arm around Kate's waist.

Kate held onto Mary's hand, and they walked out of Royce's house into a clear, star-studded Idaho night.

Becca ran to Mary and pulled the little girl into her arms. "Thank you, oh, thank you," she cried and hugged her daughter to her.

Rachel reached out for Lyla, who went to her mother and clung to her, crying.

By the time the police arrived, the Brotherhood Protectors had the men lined up and cooperating. With their leader subdued and sequestered in the same cell he'd locked Kate and Rachel in, the others didn't protest. They laid down their weapons and waited for the sheriff to arrive.

Along with the local sheriff's department came the state police and a contingent from the ATF.

Hank had his men ground their weapons before the authorities arrived to make certain no one got trigger-happy and started firing at the Brotherhood Protectors, thinking they were the bad guys.

For the next few hours, Hank fielded most of the questions, while buses were brought in to take the women and children to shelters.

"It'll take the authorities a long time to sort through everything Royce has done," Chuck said.

Kate nodded. "And longer still for those touched by his madness to recover." Her heart ached.

Her sister sat on the ground with her daughter. Someone had brought out a blanket and wrapped them in it. Rachel rocked back and forth as she held Lyla who'd fallen asleep in her arms.

"She'll need time," Kate said. "Despite how badly Myles had treated her, she was still shocked that Royce had killed him."

"Time and the love of her family will get her through." Chuck pulled Kate into the curve of his arm. "I'd like to be there with you to help."

Kate leaned into him, glad for his support. "I think we have room in our hearts. But are you sure? Sticking with us might come with a commitment clause." She arched an eyebrow.

Chuck laughed. "I'm one hundred percent committed. I knew it as soon as I opened my big, fat mouth and said I couldn't. Like I said, I made a mistake." He turned her to face him. "Please, forgive me and let me make it up to you."

"Don't promise anything you aren't comfortable with."

"If there's even a slim chance you could fall in love with me, I'm all in."

Kate's heart soared. "Slim chance?"

He wrapped his arms around her waist and stared down into her eyes, his reflecting the stars above. "I never thought it possible to love again, but you've proven me wrong. I never believed in love at first sight, but then I met you. I want you in my life. Forever. If it takes me the rest of my life to convince you, I will. Just say you'll give me a chance to earn your love."

Kate leaned up on her toes and pressed her lips to his. "Will you shut up?"

He frowned though his lips quirked upward at the corners. "Not exactly what I was hoping to hear."

"Because you won't let me get a word in edgewise." Kate laughed. "There is no slim chance of me loving you."

Chuck's smile faded. "Well, dang, I guess I have my work cut out for me. Just so you know, this SEAL doesn't give up easily."

Kate cupped his cheeks between her palms. "Chuck, there's no slim chance," she kissed him, "because there's a *big* chance I already love you." Then she claimed his lips, sealing her declaration with a kiss.

Duke bumped into Chuck's shoulder.

Chuck broke the kiss and looked up, frowning. "Hey, watch it."

"You two need a room?" Duke grinned.

Kujo stood beside Duke with Six sitting by his feet. "Didn't Hank give you the talk?"

Chuck frowned. "What talk?"

Hank clapped a hand on Chuck's shoulder. "The one about not falling for the client?"

Chuck pulled Kate close. "Nope. Didn't get that talk."

"Well," Hank said. "It wouldn't have done you any good." He shook his head. "You two would have found each other anyway. Can't argue with fate. Not when it comes to love."

"Nope," Kate said. "Fate has a wicked sense of humor."

"And she knows what the hell she's doing," Chuck brushed a soft kiss across Kate's lips.

"Is everyone ready to go home?"

"Yes," Kate said, already thinking of Eagle Rock as home.

"Yes," Chuck said. "Though I loaned the cottage to Mrs. Turner. We might have company."

Kate smiled. "We'll have a full house with my sister and Lyla moving in until they can get settled in a new life."

"That's all right by me," Chuck said. "Looks like we need to find a bigger place."

"Yes, we do. And I'm looking forward to spending more time with my family." Kate opened her arms.

Rachel rose from the ground with Lyla and walked into Kate's hug. "I love you, sis."

Kate hugged her sister tightly. "I love you, too. And by the way, have you met the man in my life? This is Chuck."

Rachel smiled up at Chuck. "No, we haven't officially met. But I like him already. Any man who can make my sister smile like that is more than okay in my book." Instead of shaking his hand, she hugged his neck. "And thank you for saving her and Lyla."

Kate couldn't stop grinning. She had her sister and her niece back in her life, and the man of her dreams loved her. Life couldn't get better.

But it did. Chuck kissed her again.

Yeah. Life did get better.

EPILOGUE

TWO MONTHS LATER...

CHUCK ADJUSTED the heat on the grill as he stood on the back porch of the house he and Kate had purchased within a week of returning to Eagle Rock. It was a rustic cedar and river stone, two-story structure with huge picture windows overlooking the foothills of the Crazy Mountains.

As soon as he and Kate had seen it, they fell in love with it and made an offer. A month later, they were all moved in and starting a life together.

Rachel and Lyla had moved in with them until Rachel could find work and save enough money to get a place of her own. Which meant Kate and Chuck got to spend more time with Rachel and Lyla.

And Lyla was thriving. She loved having an uncle

who gave her piggyback rides and the equivalent of two mothers to spoil her.

"I take it you and Kate are happy together," Hank said. He sat back in an Adirondack chair, a beer in his hand.

Sadie was helping Rachel and Kate prepare the steaks inside.

"Couldn't be happier," Chuck said.

"Are you two going to get married?" Hank held up his hands. "Sadie told me to ask you. She's all for planning another wedding. She enjoyed helping Viper and Dallas with theirs and wants to take a crack at the next one."

With a snort, Chuck lifted his beer and drank a long swallow before answering. "I asked her. She said yes, but we haven't decided on a date."

Hank pushed to his feet. "That's great news. Congratulations." He hugged Chuck, clapping him hard on the back. "Sadie will be beside herself. I couldn't be more pleased. You seem so much happier."

"I am. I didn't know how miserable I was," Chuck said, laughing, "until I wasn't."

"So, I take it you'll be staying with the Brotherhood Protectors."

Chuck nodded. "As long as you'll have me."

"Good, because I'll be taking some time off later this year, and I might need you to wrangle some of the new guys."

"I'm game."

"Most of the guys manage on their own, but I might

need you to assign cases as they come up." Hank grinned.

Chuck frowned. "Okay, what's up that you're not telling me?"

Hank's grin spread from ear to ear. "Sadie's pregnant."

It was Chuck's turn to hug and pat Hank's back. "That's great! Emma's going to have a little brother to pick on."

Hank nodded. "Or sister. We don't know what it's going to be yet. And really, I don't care. As long as Sadie and the baby are healthy, I'm happy." He shook his head. "I can't believe I'm going to be a daddy again."

Amid his happiness for Hank, Chuck couldn't help a flash of envy.

He and Kate had talked about having kids, but he was already forty-seven and Kate was thirty-six. Was it fair to bring a child into the world when they were getting older? Assuming they could even have children. His swimmers might already be dried up along with Kate's eggs.

He'd told Kate he'd be fine if they didn't have children. They would continue to be Lyla's favorite aunt and uncle. He'd told her that would be enough for him.

But hearing Hank and Sadie were expecting made Chuck wish things could have been different. He'd loved being a daddy to Sarah. And he was at a point in his life that he was willing to risk loving another child of his own. Alas, fate had her hand on the outcomes. If they were meant to have a baby, they would. If not, Chuck would be happy as long as he had Kate's love.

Sadie stepped out on the deck, carrying a tray of seasoned steaks, hotdogs and chicken breasts. She was followed by Rachel, Emma and Lyla.

"Where's Kate?" Hank asked.

"She had a little tummy upset. She'll be out in a minute," Sadie said, a small smile playing at the corners of her lips.

"Yeah, she'll be out in a minute," Rachel echoed, her lips also tipping upward. "You might want to get that food on the grill. These girls are hungry."

Emma and Lyla jumped up and down, clapping their hands.

Chuck laughed, took the tray from Sadie and went to work laying out the meat on the grill.

"By the way," he said, "I hear congratulations are in order for the Patterson family."

"Oh, Hank told you?" Sadie laid a hand across her flat belly and sat in Hank's lap. "I'm excited and can't wait to find out what we're having."

"I could wait. I like surprises," Hank said.

"I hear having two children is entirely different than having one child," Sadie said. "I look forward to the challenge."

Rachel sighed. "I always wanted two children. I didn't want Lyla to grow up an only child."

The door opened, and Kate stepped out, her face pale.

Chuck set down the spatula and hurried toward her. "Kate? Are you feeling all right?"

"No, I feel like hell." She looked at something in her

hand and then looked at him, a smile spreading across her face. "But I couldn't be better."

Chuck cupped her elbow and helped her to a chair. "I don't understand. You feel awful, but you couldn't be better?"

Sadie laughed out loud. "Don't you get it? Look at what she has in her hand. She's got morning sickness."

Chuck was so worried about Kate, he wasn't sure of what Sadie was saying. "Do I need to call a doctor? Maybe an ambulance?"

Rachel and Hank joined in Sadie's laughter.

Kate lifted the stick she had in her hand and held it in front of his face. "I'm going to be fine in nine months."

The stick, the blue line, nine months and the smile on Kate's face all added up to hit Chuck in the gut like a sucker punch.

He staggered backward, all the blood in his head draining at once.

"Catch him, he's going down!" Rachel cried.

Hank dove for Chuck and looped one of his arms over his shoulder. "You might want to save the passing out for when you're in the delivery room. It's better to have trained doctors and nurses around when you crack your skull on the floor." Hank chuckled. "I guess congratulations are in order all around."

"You're pregnant?" Chuck shook loose of Hank's hold and knelt beside Kate's chair. "Are you sure you're all right?"

"I'm sure. Just a little queasy." Her eyebrows dipped.

"Are you going to be okay? We talked about having kids, but now, are you happy? You're going to be a daddy."

Chuck pulled her into his arms and hugged her tight. "I've never been happier. I have you in my life, and now...a baby." He shook his head. Then a thought occurred to him. "Guess we'll be setting a wedding date."

Kate nodded. "Uh-huh."

"And we have a wedding planner, if she should choose to accept the mission." He shot a glance toward Sadie.

Sadie waggled her eyebrows. "I'm in as long as you have it before I give birth," Sadie said.

"You're on." Kate and Chuck said simultaneously.

"And here I thought life couldn't get better." His heart soaring, Chuck kissed Kate.

HELLFIRE, TEXAS

HELLFIRE SERIES BOOK #1

New York Times & USA Today
Bestselling Author

ELLE JAMES

All hell breaks loose when a firefighter
rescues a runaway

Hellfire, Texas

A Hellfire Story

NEW YORK TIMES BESTSELLING AUTHOR

ELLE JAMES

CHAPTER 1

THE HOT JULY SUN beat down on the asphalt road. Shimmering heat waves rose like mirages as Becket Grayson drove the twenty miles home to Coyote Creek Ranch outside of Hellfire, Texas. Wearing only a sweat-damp T-shirt and the fire retardant pants and boots of a firefighter, he couldn't wait to get home, strip, and dive into the pool. Although he'd have to hose down before he clouded the water with the thick layer of soot covering his body from head to toe.

The Hellfire Volunteer Firefighter Association met the first Saturday of every month for training in fire-fighting, rescues, and first responder care. Today had been particularly grueling in the late summer swelter. Old Lady Mersen graciously donated her dilapidated barn for structural fire training and rescue.

All thirty volunteers had been on hand to partici-pate. Though hot, the training couldn't have gone better. Each volunteer got a real taste of how fast an old barn would go up in flames, and just how much time they had to rescue any humans or animals inside. Some had the opportunity to exercise the use of SCBA, self-contained breathing apparatus, the masks and oxygen tanks that allowed them to enter smoke-filled buildings, limiting exposure and damage to their lungs. Other volunteers manned the fire engine and tanker truck, shuttling water from a nearby pond to the portable tank deployed on the ground. They unloaded a total of five tanks onto the barn fire before it was completely extinguished. With only one tanker truck, the shuttle operation slowed their ability to put out the fire, as the blaze rebuilt each time they ran out of water in the holding pool. They needed at least two tanker trucks in operation to keep the water flowing. As small as the Hellfire community was, the first engine and tanker truck would never have happened without generous donations from everyone in the district *and* a government grant. But, they had an engine that could carry a thousand, and a tanker capable of thirty-five hundred gallons. Forty-five hundred gallons was better than nothing.

Hot, tired, and satisfied with what he'd learned about combating fire without the advantages of a city fire hydrant and unlimited water supply, Becket had learned one thing that day. Firefighting involved a lot more than he'd ever imagined. As the Fire Chief said, all fires were different, just like people were different. Experience taught you the similarities, but you had to expect the unexpected.

Two miles from his turnoff, Becket could almost

taste the ice-cold beer waiting in the fridge and feel the cool water of the ranch swimming pool on his skin.

A puff of dark smoke drifted up from a stalled vehicle on the shoulder of the road ahead. The puff grew into a billowing cloud, rising into the air.

Becket slowed as he neared the disabled vehicle.

A black-haired woman stood in the V of the open driver's door, attempting to push the vehicle off the road. She didn't need to worry about getting it off the road so much as getting herself away from the smoke and fire before the gas tank ignited and blew the car to pieces.

A hundred yards away from the potential disaster, Becket slammed on his brakes, shifted into park, and jumped out of his truck. "Get away from the car!" he yelled, running toward the idiot woman. "Get away before it explodes!"

The woman shot a brief glance back at him before continuing on her mission to get the car completely off the road and into the bone-dry grass.

Becket ran up behind her, grabbed her around the middle, and hauled her away from the now-burning vehicle.

"Let go of me!" she screamed, tearing at his hands. "I have to get it off the road."

"Damn it, lady, it's not safe." Not knowing when the tank would ignite, he didn't have time to argue. Becket spun her around, threw her over his shoulder in a fireman's carry, and jogged away from the burning vehicle.

"I have to get it off the road," she said, her voice breaking with each jolt to her gut.

"Leave it where it is. I'll call in the fire department, they'll have the fire out before you know it. In the meantime, that vehicle is dangerous." He didn't stop or put her down until he was back behind his truck.

He set her on her feet, but she darted away from him, running back toward the vehicle, her long, jet-black hair flying out behind her.

Becket lunged, grabbed her arm, and jerked her back. "Are you crazy?"

"I can't leave it in the road," she sobbed. "Don't you see? He'll find it. He'll find me!" She tried prying his fingers free of her arm.

He wasn't letting go.

"The fire will ignite the gas tank. Unless you want to be fried like last year's turkey, you need to stand clear." He held her back to his chest, forcing her to view the fire and the inherent danger.

She sagged against him, her body shaking with the force of her sobs. "I have to hide it."

"Can I trust you to stay put?"

She nodded, her hair falling into her face.

"I'm making a call to the Hellfire Volunteer Fire-fighters Association."

Before he finished talking, she was shaking her head. "No. You can't. No one can know I'm here."

"Why?" He settled his hands on her shoulders and was about to turn her to face him when an explosion rocked the ground.

Becket grabbed the woman around the waist.

She yelped and whimpered as Becket ducked behind

the tailgate of his pickup, and waited for the debris to settle. Then he slowly rose.

Smoke and fire shot into the air. Where the car had been now was a raging inferno. Black smoke curled into the sky.

"Sweetheart, I won't have to call 911. In the next fifteen minutes, this place will be surrounded by firefighters."

Her head twisted left and right as she attempted to pry his hands away from her waist. "You're hurting me."

He released her immediately. "The sheriff will want a statement from you."

"No. I can't." Again, she darted away from him. "I have to get as far away from here as possible."

Becket snagged her arm again and whipped her around. "You can't just leave the scene of a fire. There will be an investigation." He stared down at her, finally getting a look at her. "Do I know you?"

"I don't..." The young woman glanced up, eyes narrowing. She reached up a hand and rubbed some of the soot off his face. Recognition dawned and her eyes grew round. "Becket? Becket Grayson?"

He nodded. "And I know I should know you, but I can't quite put my finger on it."

Her widened eyes filled with tears, and she flung her arms around his neck. "Oh, dear God. Becket!"

He held her, struggling to remember who she was.

Her body trembled, her arms like clamps around his neck.

"Hey." Surprised by her outburst, Becket patted her back. "It's going to be okay."

"No, it's not," she cried into his sweat-dampened shirt, further soaking it with her tears. "No, it's not."

His heart contracted, feeling some of the pain in her voice. "Yes, it is. But you have to start by telling me who you are." He hugged her again, then loosened the arms around his neck and pushed her to arms' length. "Well?"

The cheek she'd rested against his chest was black with soot, her hair wild and tangled. Familiar green eyes, red-rimmed and awash with tears, looked up at him. "You don't remember me." It was a statement, not a question.

"Sorry. You look awfully familiar, but I'm just not making the connection." He smiled gently. "Enlighten me."

"I'm Kinsey Phillips. We used to be neighbors."

His confusion cleared, and he grinned. "Little Kinsey Phillips? The girl who used to hang out with Nash and follow us around the ranch, getting into trouble?"

Sniffling, she nodded.

Becket shook his head and ran his gaze over her from head to toe. "Look at you, all grown up." He chuckled. "Although, you didn't get much taller."

She straightened to her full height. "No. Sadly, I stopped growing taller when I was thirteen."

"Well, Little Kinsey…" He pulled her into the curve of his arm and faced the burning mess that had been her car. "What brings you back to Hellfire? Please tell me you didn't come to have your car worked on by my brother, Rider. I'm afraid there's no hope for it."

She bit her lip, and the tremors of a few moments

before returned. "I didn't know where else to go. But I think I've made a huge mistake."

Her low, intense tone made Becket's fists clench, ready to take on whatever had her so scared. "Why do you say that?"

"He'll find me and make me pay."

"Who will find you?" Becket demanded, turning her to face him again.

She looked up at him, her bottom lip trembling. "My ex-boyfriend."

KINSEY SHUDDERED, her entire body quaking with the magnitude of what she'd done. She'd made a bid for freedom. If she didn't distance herself from the condemning evidence, all of her efforts to escape the hell she'd lived in for the past year, would be for nothing.

Sirens sounded in the distance, shaking her out of her stupor and spurring her to action. "You can't let them question me." She turned toward the still-burning vehicle. "It's bad enough this is the first place he'll look for me."

"Who is your boyfriend?"

"Ex-boyfriend," Kinsey corrected. "Dillon Massey."

"Name's familiar. Is he from around here?"

Kinsey shook her head, scanning the immediate area. "No, he's from Waco. He played football for Baylor a couple years ago, and he's playing for the Cowboys now."

"Massey, the quarterback?"

"Yes." She nodded, and then grabbed Becket's hands. "Please, you can't let anyone know I'm here. Dillon will make them think I'm crazy, and that I need him to look out for me." Kinsey pulled herself up straight. "I'm not. I've never been more lucid in my life. I had to get away."

Becket frowned. "Why?"

She raised her blouse, exposing the bruises on her ribs. "And there are more. Everywhere most people won't see."

His brows dipping lower, Becket's nostrils flared. "Bastard."

"You have no idea." Kinsey glanced toward the sound of the sirens. "Please. Let me hide. I can't face anyone."

"Who does the car belong to?"

Her jaw tightened. "Me. I'm surprised it got me this far. The thing has barely been driven in over a year."

"Why not?"

"He parked it in his shed and hid the keys. I found them early this morning, while he was passed out drunk."

"When they conduct the investigation, they'll trace the license plates."

She tilted her chin. "I removed them."

"Did you leave a purse with your identification inside the vehicle?"

"No. I didn't bring anything. I knew I'd have to start over with a new name."

"If there's anything left of the Vehicle Identification Number, they can track it through the system."

Glancing at the empty road, the sirens sounding closer, Kinsey touched Becket's arm. "It will take time for them to find the details. By then, I could be halfway across the country. But right now, I can't talk to the sheriff or the firemen. If anyone knows I'm here, that knowledge could find its way into some police database and will allow Dillon to locate me. He has connections with the state police, the district courts, and who knows what other organizations." She shook her head. "I won't go back to him."

"Okay, okay." Becket rounded to the passenger side and opened the door. "Get in."

She scrambled in, hands shaking, her heart beating so fast she was sure it would explode like the car. Kinsey glanced out the back window of the truck. The road was still clear. A curve hid them from view for a little longer. "Hurry."

"On it." Dillon fired up the engine and pulled onto the blacktop, flooring the accelerator. They reached the next curve before the rescue vehicles appeared.

Kinsey collapsed against the seat back, her nerves shot and her stomach roiling. "That was close."

"Sweetheart, you don't know just how close. If emergency vehicles hadn't been coming, I would not have left. As dry as it's been, a fire like that could spread too easily, consuming thousands of acres if left unchecked."

"I'm sorry. I wouldn't have asked you to leave the scene, but I know Dillon. The last time I tried to leave, I was caught because he called the state police and had me hauled home."

"Couldn't you have gone to a hospital and asked for a social worker to verify your injuries?" Becket glanced her way, his brows furrowed in a deep V. "Women's shelters are located all over Dallas."

"I tried." She turned toward the window, her heart hurting, reliving the pain of the beating he'd given her when he'd brought her home. He'd convinced the hospital she'd fallen down the stairs. No one wanted to believe the quarterback of an NFL team would terrorize his girlfriend into submission, beating her whenever he felt like it. "Look, you don't need to be involved in this. If you could take me to the nearest truck stop, I'll hitch a ride."

"Where would you go?"

"Wherever the trucker is going."

He shook his head. "Hitchhiking is dangerous."

Kinsey snorted. "It'd be a cakewalk compared to what I've been through."

Becket sat silent, gripping the steering wheel so tightly his knuckles turned white. "Nash is part of the sheriff's department in Hellfire now. Let me call him."

"No!" She shook her head, violently. "You can't report me to the sheriff's department. I told you. Dillon has friends everywhere, even in the state police and Texas Rangers. He'd have them looking for me. If a report popped up anywhere in the state, they'd notify him immediately."

"When was the last time he saw you?"

"Last night. After he downed a fifth of whiskey, Dillon gave me the bruises you saw. I'm sure he slept it off by eight this morning. He'll be looking for me. By now, he's got the state police on the lookout for my car.

He probably reported it as stolen. I wouldn't be surprised if he puts out a missing person report, claiming I've been kidnapped." Kinsey sighed. "Take me to the truck stop. I won't have you arrested for helping me."

"I'm not taking you to the truck stop."

Kinsey slid the window down a crack and listened. She couldn't hear the sirens anymore. Her pulse slowed and she allowed herself to relax against the back of the seat.

Becket slowed and turned at the gate to the Coyote Creek Ranch.

The entrance was just as she remembered. Rock columns supported the huge arched sign with the name of the ranch burned into the wood. She'd grown up on the much-smaller ranch next door. The only child of older parents, she'd ride her horse to visit the Graysons. She loved Nash and Rider like the brothers she'd never had. Chance had been a wild card, away more than he was there, and Becket…

As a young teen, Kinsey had the biggest crush on Becket, the oldest of the Graysons. She'd loved his longish blond hair and those startling blue eyes. Even now, covered in soot, his eyes were a bright spot of color on an otherwise-blackened face.

"I can't stay here," she said, looking over her shoulder. "Your wife and children don't need me dragging them through whatever Dillon has in store for me. I guarantee, repercussions will be bad."

"Don't worry about the Graysons. Mom and Dad are in Hawaii, celebrating their 40th anniversary. None of us brothers are married, and Lily's too stubborn to find a man to put up with her."

"What?" Kinsey glanced his way. "Not married? Are the women in this area blind? I practically worshipped you as a child."

Becket chuckled. "I remember you following me around when Nash and Rider were busy. Seems you were always there when I brought a girl out to the ranch."

Her cheeks heated. She'd done her darnedest to be in the way of Becket and his girlfriends. She didn't like it when he kissed and hugged on them. In her dreams, she'd been the one he'd fallen in love with and wanted to marry. But that hadn't happened. He'd dated the prom queen and married her soon after graduation.

"I thought you had married."

"Didn't last."

"Why not?"

"It's a long story."

"If I remember, it's a long driveway up to the ranch house."

Becket paused. For a moment, Kinsey thought he was done talking about his life and failed marriage. Then he spoke again. "After college, Briana wanted me to stay and work for one of the big architecture firms in Dallas. I was okay with the job for a while, but I missed the ranch."

"You always loved being outdoors. I can't imagine you stuck in an office."

He nodded. "Dad had a heart attack four years ago."

"I'm sorry to hear that, but I assume he survived, since they're in Hawaii."

Becket smiled. "He did, but he can't work as hard as he used to."

"So, you came home to run the ranch?"

"Yeah." Becket's gaze remained on the curving drive ahead. "Briana didn't want to leave the social scene. We tried the long-distance thing, but she didn't like it. Or rather, the marriage didn't work for her when she found a wealthy replacement for me."

"Wow. That's harsh."

"Eh. It all worked out for the best. We didn't have children, because she wanted to wait. I like it here. I have satellite internet. I telecommute in the evenings on projects for my old firm, so I stay fresh on what's going on in the industry. During the day, I'm a rancher."

"Sounds like you know what you want out of life." Kinsey sighed and rested her head against the window. "I just want to be free of Dillon."

"What about you? You went to Baylor. Did you graduate?"

"I did. With a nursing degree. I worked in pediatric nursing."

"Did you?"

"For a while. Dillon was still at Baylor when I graduated. When he signed on with the Cowboys, he changed. He said I didn't need to work and badgered me into quitting." Kinsey remembered how much she hated staying at home, and how useless she felt. "I loved my job. The kids were great."

Becket stared at the road ahead. "We leave high school with a lot of dreams and expectations."

"I figured I'd be happily married by now with one or two kids." Kinsey snorted.

"Same here." Becket's lips twisted. "We play the hands we're dealt. How long have you put up with the abuse?"

"Too long." Kinsey stared out the window. "The beatings started when he signed on with the NFL. He'd take me to parties. When his teammates paid too much attention to me, he'd get jealous, drink too much, and hit me when we got back to our place."

"Why didn't you leave him then?"

"In the morning, he'd apologize and promise not to do it again." Her lip pulled back in a sneer. "But, he did. Eventually, he stopped taking me to the parties." Her life would have been so different had she left him the first time he hit her. She'd been a fool to believe he would stop.

"Couldn't you have gone to your family?"

"Each time I mentioned leaving, Dillon flew into a rage and threatened to kill me. Then he took away my car. He said it was for my own good. The car was too old, and needed too much work to drive." At first, Kinsey had thought his action was out of concern for her safety. But her checkbook and credit cards disappeared, and he blamed her for being careless, forcing her to live off whatever pittance of cash he gave her. Without a job, she had no income and became a prisoner in Dillon's home. "He told me I was a terrible driver and shouldn't be on the road. That I'd probably end up crashing into someone."

"The man's a dick."

"Tell me about it." Kinsey bit her lip to keep it from trembling. "I think part of the reason he stopped me from driving was that I'd go to visit my parents. Like he was jealous of how much I loved them, and liked spending time at home. By taking away my car, he left me with no way of getting there. Mom and Dad came up to visit me in Dallas when they could, but after they left, Dillon would stomp around the house, sullen and angry. He'd accuse me of being a mama's girl. If I defended myself, he hit me."

"Your parents were good people," Becket said. "I was sorry to hear of the accident."

Tears slipped from Kinsey's eyes. "They were on their way to visit me, since I couldn't go to them. I think they knew I was in trouble."

"Why didn't you tell them what was going on?"

"I was embarrassed, ashamed, and scared. By then, Dillon was my world. I didn't think I had any other alternatives. And he swore he loved me."

"He had a lousy way of showing it," Becket said through tight lips.

She agreed. Along with the physical abuse, Dillon heaped enough mental and verbal abuse on Kinsey, she'd started to believe him.

You're not smart enough to be a nurse. You'll kill a kid with your carelessness, he'd say.

When her parents died, she'd stumbled around in a fog of grief. Dillon coerced her into signing a power of

213

attorney, allowing him to settle their estate. Before she knew what he'd done, he'd sold her parents' property, lock, stock and barrel, without letting her go through any of their things. He'd put the money in his own account, telling her it was a joint account. She never saw any of the money—never had access to the bank.

Several times over the past few months, she had considered leaving him. But with her parents gone, no money to start over, and no one to turn to, she'd hesitated.

Then, a month ago, he'd beaten her so badly she'd been knocked unconscious. When she came to, she knew she had to get out before he killed her. She stole change out of Dillon's drawer, only a little at a time so he wouldn't notice. After a couple weeks, she had enough for a tank of gas.

Dillon settled into a pattern of drinking, beating her, and passing out. She used the hours he was unconscious to scour the house in search of her keys. She'd begun to despair, thinking he'd thrown them away. Until last night. He'd gone out drinking with his teammates. When he'd arrived home, he'd gone straight to the refrigerator for another beer. He'd forgotten he'd finished off the last bottle the night before and blamed her for drinking the beer. With no beer left in the house, he reached for the whiskey.

With a sickening sense of the inevitable, Kinsey braced herself, but she was never prepared when he started hitting. This time, when he passed out, she'd raided his pockets and the keychain he guarded carefully. On it was the key to her car.

Grabbing the handful of change she'd hoarded, she didn't bother packing clothes, afraid if she took too long, he'd wake before she got her car started and out of the shed.

Heart in her throat, she'd pried open the shed door and climbed into her dusty old vehicle. She'd stuck the key in the ignition, praying it would start. Dillon had charged the battery and started the car the week before, saying it was time to sell it. Hopefully, the battery had retained its charge.

On her second attempt, she pumped the gas pedal and held her breath. The engine groaned, and by some miracle it caught, coughed, and sputtered to life.

Before she could chicken out, before Dillon could stagger through the door and drag her out of the vehicle, she'd shoved the gear shift into reverse and backed out of the shed, scraping her car along the side of Dillon's pristine four-wheel drive pickup, and bounced over the curb onto the street.

She'd made it out, and she wasn't going back.

ABOUT THE AUTHOR

ELLE JAMES also writing as MYLA JACKSON is a *New York Times* and *USA Today* Bestselling author of books including cowboys, intrigues and paranormal adventures that keep her readers on the edges of their seats. With over eighty works in a variety of sub-genres and lengths she has published with Harlequin, Samhain, Ellora's Cave, Kensington, Cleis Press, and Avon. When she's not at her computer, she's traveling, snow skiing, boating, or riding her ATV, dreaming up new stories. Learn more about Elle James at www.ellejames.com

Website | Facebook | Twitter | GoodReads | Newsletter |
BookBub | Amazon
Or visit her alter ego Myla Jackson at mylajackson.com
Website | Facebook | Twitter | Newsletter

Follow Me!
www.ellejames.com
ellejames@ellejames.com

ALSO BY ELLE JAMES

SEAL'S Desire (#2)

SEAL's Embrace (#3)

SEAL's Obsession (#4)

SEAL's Proposal (#5)

SEAL's Seduction (#6)

SEAL'S Defiance (#7)

SEAL's Deception (#8)

SEAL's Deliverance (#9)

Hearts & Heroes Series

Wyatt's War (#1)

Mack's Witness (#2)

Ronin's Return (#3)

Sam's Surrender (#4)

Ballistic Cowboy

Hot Combat (#1)

Hot Target (#2)

Hot Zone (#3)

Hot Velocity (#4)

Texas Billionaire Club

Tarzan & Janine (#1)

Something To Talk About (#2)

Who's Your Daddy (#3)

Love & War (#4)

Hellfire Series

Hellfire, Texas (#1)

Justice Burning (#2)

Smoldering Desire (#3) TBD

Up in Flames (#4) TBD

Plays with Fire (#5) TBD

Hellfire in High Heels (#6) TBD

Cajun Magic Mystery Series

Voodoo on the Bayou (#1)

Voodoo for Two (#2)

Deja Voodoo (#3)

Cajun Magic Mysteries Books 1-3

Billionaire Online Dating Service

The Billionaire Husband Test (#1)

The Billionaire Cinderella Test (#2)

The Billionaire Bride Test (#3) TBD

The Billionaire Matchmaker Test (#4) TBD

SEAL Of My Own

Navy SEAL Survival

Navy SEAL Captive

Navy SEAL To Die For

Navy SEAL Six Pack

Devil's Shroud Series

Deadly Reckoning (#1)

Deadly Engagement (#2)

Deadly Liaisons (#3)

Deadly Allure (#4)

Deadly Obsession (#5)

Deadly Fall (#6)

Covert Cowboys Inc Series

Triggered (#1)

Taking Aim (#2)

Bodyguard Under Fire (#3)

Cowboy Resurrected (#4)

Navy SEAL Justice (#5)

Navy SEAL Newlywed (#6)

High Country Hideout (#7)

Clandestine Christmas (#8)

Thunder Horse Series

Hostage to Thunder Horse (#1)

Thunder Horse Heritage (#2)

Thunder Horse Redemption (#3)

Christmas at Thunder Horse Ranch (#4)

Demon Series

Hot Demon Nights (#1)

Demon's Embrace (#2)

Tempting the Demon (#3)

Lords of the Underworld

Witch's Initiation (#1)

Witch's Seduction (#2)

The Witch's Desire (#3)

Possessing the Witch (#4)

Stealth Operations Specialists (SOS)

Nick of Time

Alaskan Fantasy

Blown Away

Made in the USA
Las Vegas, NV
06 January 2022

40650314R00127